To Sonia

ALL AT SEA

by

Joy Burnett

Best Wishes
Joy Burnett

License Notes

Published by Joy Burnett, author of 'On the Loose'.

Copyright 2016 Joy Burnett

***

Acknowledgements

Thanks to my editor, Morgen Bailey, who has encouraged, helped and advised me and has edited this book.

And especially to those on the Caribbean cruise who inspired some of the stories within this collection.

***

With up to two thousand passengers on the big liners, an average of nine hundred staff and crew, and with no policing on board and floating in international waters, disappearances are frequent and often uninvestigated.

Cruise ships are thought of as a luxury getaway from our busy or monotonous lifestyles, an escape from the drudgery of cooking and cleaning, and a chance to dress up, learn new skills, to be entertained and to explore faraway places. On these family-friendly floating paradises a woman is twice as likely to be sexually assaulted, and robbery on board ship and on the islands is fairly commonplace.

Death is the last thing anyone expects on a holiday cruise ship but the truth is that about 400 people each year vanish for various reasons including murder, suicides, accidents and mysterious disappearances. And all with no police to investigate or prevent crime and no immediate help available.

Sickness, fire, malfunction, running aground, and the forces of nature make them a vulnerable place to be.

These stories while inspired by real events have been written to be entertaining and uplifting, and whilst there are dangers, it is a light-hearted look at the pleasures of cruising.

CONTENTS

ANGELA – The Cruise Angel

"Go three times around the deck and that'll be one mile. OK, Let's get started ladies!" shouted Angela, whistle in hand and dressed in her best royal blue velour trackie. She stood beaming, ready to lead her group of single ladies on their first exercise of the cruise. That morning, she had contacted everyone to see if they fancied getting together for the walk as the sun was shining for the first time since leaving Southampton. The decks were closed to everyone because of February's bad weather. The great cruiser had rocked and rolled for three days solid and many on board had succumbed to staying in their cabins. Today, the sun peeped through the clouds and the gale-force winds subsided, so the 'fresh air-deprived' were out in force, marching along the decks. One or two stalwarts sat gazing out to sea with their open books flapping in the wind.

Fifteen singletons had turned up for the walk, all ladies.

"Where are our gentlemen?" inquired Angela who had put herself in charge of the 'singles' on the cruise when they had all met up on the first day.

"They are watching some 'footie' match. All five of them." grinned Edna, another veteran cruiser, who was at least ninety years old. Wrapped in a great pink pashmina, and taking deep breaths of damp sea air, she was about to do her daily mile, a sadly missed essential due to the bad weather.

"It's no wonder they die before us, eh?" sniffed Angela. The ladies laughed and with headscarves flying, hands tucked into pockets and determined looks all round, they set off.

Greta, a delightful, just-retired, Swedish lady had volunteered to push Betty around in her wheelchair. Even though it was motorised, the decks were rather slippery, and Betty was nervous.

Angela marched ahead singing, "Ain't it a glorious day, bright as a morning in May," regardless of the fact that it *was* February, still very windy and despite the sunshine, the heavens threatened to open again at any minute.

Angela and her husband Harry had been veteran cruisers, and when Harry died suddenly three years before, Angela was lost. They had been together for forty-three years and had had a good and rewarding life. She was only sixty-six and renowned for her outgoing and exuberant personality and having Harry by her side, she was never short of a listening ear, an encouraging smile or a hand to hold. They had only ever spent a single night apart, when Harry was stuck in Aberdeen on a business trip and the flight back to Teesside had been cancelled because of snowstorms.

After Harry died, Angela's days alone became long and dreary, and she found herself doing less and less. They hadn't a family or pets, had relied on each other *so* much, had not made or needed many friends, and now Angela found herself unprepared to go out with those they had, or even on her own. When the time came to sort out Harry's papers, she heaved a great sigh, took a box of tissues and shut herself in his little office; the third bedroom, converted years ago when he started working from home and began the task. With old bank statements, lists, receipts and letters consigned to the bin, she worked on the pending file and that's where she found the holiday bookings. Harry loved to surprise her with the holidays he'd planned. He always knew where she wanted to go and when. Being such an organised person, he'd planned their next three years holidays in advance.

Harry spoke fluent French and planned to take Angela to Paris for her birthday in April, then drive down to Cannes and Monte Carlo.

Definitely not, I'd hate doing that on my own. So she set about cancelling the holiday in France, a weekend break in the Lake District, and the Christmas market trip to Bruges.

It was then she found the three bookings for cruises, one to the Mediterranean, one to the Black Sea and another to the Caribbean.

No, I'm not going anywhere without him, she thought, *it just wouldn't be the same. I'll cancel everything.* But flicking through the pages, Angela found a sealed envelope attached to one of the ticket instructions.

Opening it carefully, she read, *Today I have been diagnosed with terminal cancer and it is unlikely that I will make all of these holidays. Nevertheless, Angela, my darling, you must go on them. We've had so much fun together and I will be with you in spirit wherever you go. So many people do go on their own, and I know you could have a wonderful time. You bring so much fun and joy into people's lives (mostly mine of course), that it would be a sin to deprive others of your infectious laugh and constant good humour. Enjoy making others as happy as you have made me. H xxxxxxx*

Tears had streamed down Angela's face.

Oh Harry, she thought, *how clever you are.*

After much consideration, Angela decided that she *would* go after all. She knew most of the P&O ships quite well. Since she and Harry had retired, they had been on at least five cruises and were well aware that lots of people did travel on their own. Having said that, several years before Angela had met a single lady on the way to South America who hadn't been out of her cabin more than twice in six days and Angela was determined that would never happen to her or anyone else on the cruises she went on.

On the first single's coffee morning organised by the rather young entertainment manager Heidi, Angela became aware of just how many people *were* actually on their own. Jack, Annabelle, Edna, Gregory, Esmeralda, Kitty, May and many more, all intent on getting their money's worth as cruising was not cheap for singletons.

The different activities on the ship meant that there was something for everyone but lots of them *were* for couples only, so Angela decided that she would make sure everyone could get involved in something especially for them, and not feel left out or lonely. She volunteered to organise a bridge group, a general knowledge quiz, and a cake decorating morning just specifically for the singles on board. Several small groups were going to do the shore excursions together when they reached the Caribbean islands. Angela knew how daunting they could be on your own. She arranged help for Betty in her wheelchair and Jack Edwards who wanted to learn to dance, but was too shy to ask anyone to partner him.

"So kind," he muttered after Angela had asked

everyone, and three ladies had volunteered.

"You are our cruise angel," said Mavis, after a fantastic afternoon spent on a 50s / 60s quiz game that Angela had devised. Everyone had joined in and laughed as they remembered their teenage days.

"Never enjoyed myself so much," Mavis said. "I've completely forgotten all about feeling seasick and the terrible weather. Thank you so much, Angela."

"Yes, thank you so much. You have made this cruise such fun," added Betty

"I agree. Thank you, Angela," said Jack.

"My pleasure," she replied. It meant so much to her to see all the happy faces and to know that she had contributed to their pleasure and their holiday. *Thank you, Harry.*

***

AVADHUT – New Boy

"Where are we now?" demanded the whiskered, overweight gentleman standing gazing out to sea. Avadhut had no idea at all. He was busy hurrying along the lower deck trying to locate the blonde in the yellow Kaftan who had ordered the cocktail of the day; a rather disgusting mix of something blue, vodka, elderberry flower and lemonade. He had only been on this ship a matter of days and wasn't even sure where they were headed. Avadhut had never been out of India before and he had arrived in Southampton on a coach from Heathrow after a long, tiring flight, and directed immediately to the enormous ship. This was his fourth or fifth day, he wasn't quite sure, and here he was being asked a question he had no idea how to answer.

He had spent six weeks on the induction course in P&O's office and recruitment centre in Mumbai. None of it covered identifying where they happened to be when on the great ocean. It was taking him all his time to stay upright as there was no induction that mimicked the rolling waves that had been attacking the ship since they had left Southampton.

His priority was to do as he was ordered and serve the one thousand nine hundred and eighty-two passengers to the best of his ability, and with the widest smile possible. After nine months of cruising, he could return to Mumbai and he would get three months leave. What could possibly be better than that? He would then get married to Layla as now he could afford to; his salary was more that he had ever dreamed. He knew he would be able to save a great deal as he only had very brief shore time and there was little to do on the ship in the spare time he did have. There was a crew bar below deck but Avadhut didn't drink alcohol.

"I am sorry sir, I do not know, but I will find out for you," he replied to the inquiring gentleman.

Geography had not been his best subject at school and he was amazed that P&O had employed him considering his lack of knowledge of the world.

Who in heaven's name could he ask such a question of? The navigating crew and captain would know but they wouldn't take kindly to him asking. He would deliver the cocktail and disappear quickly to the Horizon bar.

At home in Mumbai, he had worked in the Taj hotel since being a teenager, moving his way up the ladder from the kitchens to the best silver service restaurant. He still lived at home with his mum and dad but his best friend Vejay had encouraged him to apply to P&O, and here Avadhut was on the same ship that Vejay had been on for the past two years.

Another friend, big, handsome Luis, who had also worked in the Mumbai Taj had been employed by P&O for five years, and of course he was now an old hand. He had been on all the ships, and was always showing off his extensive knowledge of everything, giving endless advice about on-board behaviour, how to dodge difficult passengers, who to look for when you wanted something, and all about making the best of being employed by P&O. He told Avadhut that life could be really good if you treated the passengers right, but you had to know how to identify the good tippers, those that would 'cough up' a nice big gratuity at the end of their holiday.

"Especially the older ladies on their own, Avadhut. They will reward you in more ways than one," Luis had told him with a wink, on his first day.

"That may be OK with you, Luis, but I am engaged to be married and I will remain faithful to Layla."

"But she would never know. I have been engaged to Sheveta for two years. Let me tell you, there is fun to be had. So many lonely ladies. Are we not here to keep our passengers happy? It means nothing to me and Sheveta trusts me."

Vejay was listening to their conversation whilst busily polishing his scruffy shoes. "More fool her. I know you, what you are up to? Are you trying to win the 'golden mattress' award?"

"What is this award, Luis?" asked Avadhut.

" Ha… well, it was started on the very smart ships back in the eighties and it is a secret. I cannot tell you but you must try to guess." Luis grinned. "What do you think it is?"

"Is it real, a real award?"

"No, not really, just an exercise in using your good looks and extensive charm with the lady passengers." Luis waggled his tongue in a suggestive way and nudged Avadhut in the ribs, a very male gesture that was instantly understood.

"You are very disgusting, Luis."

"How long have you been on board?" laughed Luis. "You might feel different after a few months without any female company. If it's offered on a plate, take it, Avadhut. A bird in the hand, eh... and why not."

"What are you talking about birds for Luis? I am not understanding you now."

"Aha, so this award, who do you think will win it

this year, Luis?"

"Not me, that's for sure. Not had much luck lately. Gilroy down on the cabins has struck lucky this trip though. In 314 he's got a nympho... what do they call them? Nympho... man... iac, yes, you know what I mean, one who can't get enough... "

"Really? A passenger is it, Luis?"

"Yep, she's not bad looking either, plenty of dosh, lots of good jewellery. She'll look after him if he plays right. She's called Esmeralda... could be about fifty-eight. Gilroy says she is more, and he should know I guess. He's seen bits we haven't, if you know what I mean."

Luis wrinkled his nose, and laughed. "She asked him straight out on her second night on the ship. He said no, at first. No, he couldn't possibly, but she got hold of his winkle and kissed him hard and he then said 'OK'. Been in every night since."

"I am glad I am not on the cabins then. What to do, eh?" Avadhut was beginning to wonder about life on board. A bit dangerous after all.

"You can get them in the bars too. Last year Freddie had one fall in love with him. Nice she was, bought him presents, followed him around and told him she loved him and would look after him, but she started to get into his e-mails. She sent a message to his girlfriend in Kerala saying she was going to marry him. Can you imagine that? Cocked things right up for him back home."

"I hope that won't happen to me. I am faithful to Maya. Always."

"You'll learn... you'll learn, plenty of time. Only another eight and a half months to go. You are a good-looking boy, Avadhut. Perhaps, in time you will win the 'golden mattress award'."

***

KITTY – Out of Order

Kitty was late, again, only a few minutes, which for her wasn't too bad. She burst into the dining room with enthusiastic apologies and nearly knocked the poor waiter flying. The most uncoordinated lady in the line-dancing class, she seemed to have little control over her long skinny legs, or any other part of her anatomy for that matter.

Her chair fell backward onto the waiter's toes. "Oh sorry, did I do that?" she squealed.

Avadhut smiled at Kitty even though the chair had hit his big toe; the one that had the ingrowing toenail. Swallowing hard and maintaining his smile, he finally got her seated, her napkin in place and handed her the menu. This was the fifth day of the cruise and Kitty, Jayne, May and Angela had been meeting for dinner. They were all single travellers and this was Kitty's first cruise. The 'girls,' as Angela insisted on calling them, even though their average age was about seventy, met at a regular time for dinner and spent their evenings together.

"I look terrible, don't I?" asked Kitty flicking at her feathery hair. "Such a busy day you know."

"No, you look fine." Jayne and May said in unison.

"You look lovely," Jayne added.

Neither was accurate as Kitty could have looked a lot better, but she had an unfortunate posture; shoulders permanently pushed forward as if trying to fold herself inside her chest. Small too, only about five feet, and as slender as a pre-adolescent. Clearly she had not been in God's front line for looks either. He had given her thin straight blonde hair and a narrow mouth that was permanently in a position of apology; pushed forward in an exaggerated pout. Her attempt at improving her looks consisted of a blue line drawn across her eyelids and a slash of red lipstick. She was fifty-plus but her dress was above her knees and obviously from a children's department store somewhere in Manchester where she lived. Kitty loved to be the centre of attention and she had a nervous, zingy energy that was totally beyond her control. Every movement threatened to disrupt the table, and both May and Jayne found her constant chatter not only amusing but slightly ridiculous. Angela was not so keen.

"Where's Gilbert. Has anybody seen Gilbert? Last seen? Where is he now? Oh yes... launderette, I guess. That rhymes, doesn't it... silly me. Now what are we eating tonight, ladies? she asked, as she ran her finger down the huge list of choices that were offered for dinner.

"Kitty, you're off again," laughed May.

"I know. Ridiculous, aren't I? Oh hell, shall I have the steak or gammon? No, steak is out. Off red meat, you know… what have you been up to then? Been playing bridge today, Angela?" Kitty prattled on without waiting for her questions to be answered. "Can't wait to go ashore in Barbados? I want to go to the beach. Was thinking I would take my lilo–"

"You've got a lilo?" enquired May. "Why would you bring a lilo on a cruise?"

"I bought it in case we went down, not for the beach really."

"What would you like, Madam?" interrupted Avadhut. The other ladies had already given him their dinner order and he had three other tables waiting for

20

their orders to be taken. The restaurant manager watched him. The ladies stared at Kitty. "Madam, have you decided on the gammon?"

"What's it for then?" asked May.

"I think I'll have the chicken... yes, yes and a large glass of Merlot. Oh, sorry different waiter. Could you ask?" Turning to May, she explained in the same breath. "Yes... it's in case we go down... I bought it at the last minute. Got a pump too. Trouble is, it is rather huge, didn't realise how big it was when I bought it. It has these long rods to slip along the sides. A bit difficult to put together."

Jayne laughed. "You're *not* serious?"

"Yes, I am. I just thought as it's my first cruise, I should be prepared."

"You can't be serious." Jayne repeated, conjuring up images of Kitty in the narrow corridors trying to pump up a lilo in the middle of the very well-exercised emergency procedures that were in place on the ship. By now the whole table had lost interest in the food and were laughing wildly.

"Chicken it is then, Madam?" said Avadhut moving away from the conversation before he too burst into laughter.

"I suppose you could always hire it out on the beach," laughed May.

"It's away safe now... under the bed. Anyway, have you seen Gilbert? He's been supplying my drinks, you know. I need a glass of red. That's all men are good for really, isn't it?"

Angela stopped laughing. "No actually I don't agree. I had a wonderful husband. He did far more than buy drinks for me."

"Oh well, that's what I think they are good for," said Kitty oblivious of the barb in Angela's tone. "That and a bit of the other when I have a mind, you know." She giggled. "Should have shaved my legs, just in case."

"What are you talking about?" asked May. "Have you really got a lilo under your bed?"

Kitty shuffled forward and rested her elbows on the table, disrupting the neatly set cutlery and with a serious expression explained. "I know how ridiculous it seems now but I had this friend you see, kept hinting at disasters. I couldn't sleep so I went and bought it just in case. Brought Wellingtons too. Not sure what they are for."

"You are off your trolley, Kitty. Anyway let's get off lilos, shall we? Are we going to the show tonight? Great comedian, I understand. You've seen him before haven't you, Angela?" asked May.

"Yes, he's good," replied Angela who was struck by how much she was missing Harry even though she had been alone over three years. Kitty's remark had made her think about how lovely he'd been, and how much they had appreciated and supported each other. Kitty had obviously never known that sort of relationship and Angela felt a surge of sympathy for her.

Kitty was now busy watching everyone coming into the dining room, her eyes darting this way and that, occasionally lifting her fingers to wave to someone she had met.

May was telling a story about when she was a midwife and as everyone's attention was no longer on her, Kitty participated very little in the conversation.

By the end of the meal, she was fidgeting and getting bored with the all-female company, and as soon as dinner was over, she pushed back her chair.

She would search out Gilbert. She needed a drink and the prices on the ship were far too expensive for her to be buying her own.

"I'm off," she declared. "Can't waste party time, and I need to find Gilbert." She blew exaggerated kisses to everyone.

"Poor Gilbert," said Angela as Kitty skipped off.

Gilbert was sitting waiting for Kitty in the Horizon lounge. He had been there for over an hour and had amused himself watching the couples, dressed in their smart jackets and posh frocks, going into the dining room. He wasn't hungry and having had afternoon tea, had decided to wait until Kitty came out.

Gilbert was seventy years old, not a handsome man, hard of hearing and was really quite shy. Never having married, he found any sort of conversation with women difficult. This was the main reason that Kitty was so easy to be with. She talked all the time and flirted with him in a way that no other woman ever had. He had no need to converse as long as she was there, chatting non-stop and while her glass was full, she was happy.

Gilbert was considered wealthy and over-generous by his friends but none of them took advantage of him as Kitty was doing. He knew of course, he *was* paying for all the drinks. He was quite happy watching her get drunk at his expense every night as he had twice had the pleasure of taking her back to her cabin and slowly undressing her before putting her to bed. Both times he had caressed her tiny breasts, stroked her stomach and run his fingers through her pubic hair. With the tips of his fingers he had caressed her gingery, little fanny, and the previous night as she had muttered drunkenly, he opened her legs wide.

As she slept, he had even switched the light on to examine what lay between them. Never more than that as yet. He was not even sure whether he could achieve any sort of erection good enough to go any further.

Nevertheless, on returning to his cabin with the image of Kitty spread akimbo in his head, he had managed to ejaculate for the first time in years. He had slept really well that night.

"Where have you been? I've been looking for you. We were going to get a drink before dinner. Have you had yours? Dinner? I didn't see you," said Kitty. "Come on anyway, there's a disco party in 'Le Club'."

She giggled and took his arm as if they were old friends. "Let's get trolleyed, babe."

Perhaps tonight would be the night, thought Gilbert and smiled as he led her toward the bar.

***

MARK – Second Chance

It had all started on the first day of real sunshine, after the cruise set off out of Southampton, and Carol and Mark had settled into their poolside recliners, straight after breakfast.

Lifting his eyes to watch the dappled light playing on the shimmering swimming pool, Mark could see a few brave souls, trying the water, regardless of the temperature.

It was then that he saw her.

Helena Cartwright walked across the deck toward the pool. At first he thought he must be mistaken.

Holy fuck. It can't be, can it? No, surely not, just somebody who reminded him, yet again, of the Helena he had adored. There had been many women over the years that he had spotted, sometimes followed. He had even once tapped the shoulder of a lady at the bus stop outside Sainsbury's, convinced that it was her. He had imagined meeting up with her on so many occasions. It would be at the theatre, on the underground, or perhaps in the library where she would be studying. Always, there would be a dramatic reunion. Mark imagined the rush into each other's arms, the whispered apologies and endearments. In those early days his hopes had leaped and crashed a dozen times every week.

It was only in rare moments now that he thought of Helena, and the giddy heights, they had reached together in their teens and twenties.

Now, watching this woman walking towards the pool, he knew it must be her. No one moved with such grace; she glided like a ballerina. He knew for certain when she stopped, and lifted her hair from her neck, a familiar gesture, remembered instantly. She was slimmer and more toned than he remembered, her blonde hair straighter than it had been. She was wearing a plain black swimsuit with gold trimming, elegant and expensive, and as she stepped into the pool, he caught sight of her breasts. He instantly recalled the first time he had touched them. Their parents often took holidays together, and that year they had been joined by Helena's Aunt Irene and Uncle Stan. Mark was seventeen, and Helena a year younger. Even though they had known each other all their lives, they had spent little time together. Attraction for each other was slow, and shy at first, but on that sunny day, they had wandered off away from their families picnicking on the beach, and sat behind the sand dunes.

They fell in love.

Nothing since had ever been as romantic as that day. They had lost their virginity together, not that it seemed a loss in any way to either of them. From that holiday onward, they were inseparable; they sang in the choir, played in the school orchestra and studied together. They were in love as only the young can be, completely and utterly consumed.

Helena was a tall, stunning blonde, and was studying for her A levels. Extremely clever, ambitious, and hard-working. She wrote, and directed school plays, and wanted to go to drama school to learn about all aspects of the theatre, and to work in production. Mark, on the other hand, was happy to let life take him wherever, and was pursuing the idea of singing, or perhaps playing the piano professionally. He was vague and far more relaxed about the future than Helena could ever have been.

Having been brought up in a poor district of Middlesbrough in a family who had little in the way of luxuries, Helena was determined that her life would be successful *and* wealthy. Mark's family were far better off. The two families had been friends since their own school days, even though Mark's family had moved to a considerably smarter part of town.

Interrupting his thoughts, Carol – Mark's fiancée – said, "Isn't it lovely today. I'm so happy to be having this break with you. It's like a pre-honeymoon. Are you going to read, Mark?"

"Mmm," he muttered, still intent on gazing at Helena. She looked stunning, moving in a steady crawl towards him.

Long-forgotten memories flooded back.

At eighteen, Mark had moved to the London and joined the London School of Music, found a bedsit in Camden town, and Helena had arrived less than a year later. Working hard, Mark gained several grades in his piano, his vocal training had intensified, and he was sure that he wanted to pursue a career in opera. To make ends meet, he and three other aspiring musicians sung together as a group. At the time, when rock and roll was all most young men thought about, Mark was singing classical arias on the streets of London. Busking made them extra pocket money, and as a group they were really exceptional.

Mark and Helena were so happy to be together, making love everywhere and at every opportunity. Memories flooded back; her funky clothes, the way she held her cigarettes, her long smooth legs, her penchant for spicy, heady perfume, her tendency to forget to eat or buy food. But most of all, he remembered the passion of their sex together; endlessly inventive, exciting, and all-consuming. Mark felt his penis flicker as he remembered.

Carol interrupted his thoughts, "Shall I put some cream on your back. You don't want to burn."

"Mmm, yes OK."

"Lean forward a bit, There we are… that's better." Carol slowly massaged Mark's back and shoulders and as she finished, she leaned forward to kiss the top of his head.

Mark turned briefly to thank her.

By then, Helena had swam the length of the pool several times, and was climbing out at the far end. He watched, and became mesmerised, by the sparkling water that clung to her shoulders and back. *She must be sixty-plus now and she's still stunningly beautiful,* he thought as she walked away. Mark could feel panic rising as she moved out of site. *What if I don't see her again? Perhaps she's with her husband, partner or friends.* Mark felt compelled to find out. So many years had passed and so much had changed for him, he would be surprised if she even recognised him. In his youth, he had been dark and handsome, with a strong athletic body, and wrinkle-free skin that tanned easily.

To that day he didn't know what had happened to her, or where she had gone when she had disappeared, that fateful summer. It was more than likely that she had left him for someone else, but at the time he had refused to believe so. She had not only left him, but her theatre course, her family, her friends and practically everything she owned. She had just disappeared with their savings and her newly-acquired passport. They had been planning to backpack around France in the summer recess.

Mark's parents had died relatively young so the link with the families had also gone, and none of their existing friends had heard from her.

Five years later, he had married Kate, who was lovely: kind, attractive and charming, and they had had two beautiful, now grown-up, children.

Rising quickly, and apologising to Carol, Mark indicated the direction of the toilets. She nodded and went back to her book.

Helena had disappeared around the corner to the aft deck. As he turned the corner, he hesitated, and watched her heading for a solitary recliner looking out to sea. His heart was beating fast, and he realised he was holding his breath.

She turned as she was adjusting her towel.

Slowly, lifting her sunglasses, Helena realised who it was standing just a few feet away from her. She too caught her breath, and thought to deny him, but also knew that anonymity on board was almost impossible.

"Ahh." She made a small, almost imperceptible sound.

"Helena."

"Mark. Well I never."

"Are you alone?"

"Yes."

A moment's silence followed, while both tried to decide how to start a conversation after over forty years? A statement or a question?

Mark looked as if he wanted to ask the question, but after so long, perhaps it was inappropriate to want to know why she had left him without an explanation all those years before.

A wave of regret passed through Helena, but also a flutter of happiness pushed its way into her thoughts. *Perhaps, just perhaps, she was getting another chance.* Maybe, he wouldn't ask. She knew that she would never be able to explain what had motivated her departure.

Mark was smiling at her.

"It's been a long time. Are you on your own?" she asked.

"I'm with a friend... Carol, my fiancée, actually."

"Oh, right." Helena's disappointment was obvious.

"You are looking well... Perhaps we could have a drink together, catch up... for old time's sake. Just the two of us. Yes?" Mark suggested.

At that moment, he couldn't imagine introducing her to Carol.

"Yes, that would be good." Helena replied, looking relieved, that she would have time to think about what she would say.

"The Magnum bar? Say about eleven-thirty, after the shows have finished?"

Helena nodded.

"Lovely. See you later." Mark was elated, and hurried off to the men's toilet where he peed out his tension with a happy grin on his face.

Helena was in the bar waiting at eleven-thirty as Mark and Carol made their way toward their cabin.

"You go on up." Mark said. "I think I might just have a nightcap. Would you like me to bring you one up?" Mark tried to be as casual as he could.

"How sweet you are," Carol replied as she wrapped her arms around him. "No thanks, darling, I am going to sleep well, after so much fresh air today. Don't be long."

That evening, they had both dressed carefully, thinking about their planned rendezvous. It was the ship's 'smart' evening, so Mark had put on his best dark grey suit, with a soft lemon shirt, and a mustard, lemon and grey striped tie, carefully chosen. Helena was wearing a striking black sheath with a shimmering, black beaded butterfly across her breast, long jet and diamond earrings, and heels that would normally only be worn if she was assured of a seat.

Tonight, they were lucky, and Vejay, one of the waiters, ushered them to a quiet corner away from the bar.

They caught up, like old friends, laughing and chatting, confiding their achievements and disappointments. Helena told Mark briefly about her marriages, her lack of children, her friends, and returning to see her family after years abroad. How Uncle Stan had run off with a barmaid, Aunt Irene couldn't have been happier. Helena and Mark laughed at family stories and silly incidents.

'Do you remember when, or how, or somebody' kept their conversation light and safe, until Mark asked seriously, "What happened to us?"

31

Helena looked at him and wondered too. His hair was grey, but he was still a very attractive and desirable man. He had thickened around the middle and he stooped, which made him look shorter than she remembered.

She answered him carefully. "I don't know really. Over the years, I have often looked back, and thought it was all a bad dream."

"Thanks," Mark said huffily.

"No, no, I didn't mean when we were together. I didn't say that to hurt your feelings, I meant the break up." Helena shifted uncomfortably in her chair. "It had just gone wrong, and we were fighting *all* the time. It's a long time ago, and I don't know when it started, but we suddenly seemed to want different things. I wanted more; to travel, have a career and earn lots of money, and you wanted to settle down and have babies."

"I wanted you."

"And I wanted *you* to take earning a living more seriously, stop busking and... oh I don't know... be a bit more ambitious."

"We did well, you know. Sang at the Palace once, at a private party for Lady Diana."

"Really?"

"Yes. We were good too. We did well as a group and as individuals; toured, worked with all the great orchestras, even did La Scala a couple of times. Although I'm semi-retired now, I still have my own recording studio – Leewards Music – you might have heard of it." Mark hesitated. "Can I ask you a question?"

Suddenly the night air seemed to cool, and Helena wondered how she could ever explain. She knew he was going to ask why she left, without a word, but, he asked instead, "Why did you never contact me again? We had, after all, been together more than four years. I thought we were friends, as well as… you know, lovers."

"I was afraid to. I thought you might hate me."

"No."

"I was selfish and ambitious, and wanted more than I thought you could give me. I never wanted to settle down and have children."

Mark nodded as though he understood everything, when in fact, Helena thought the opposite was probably true. Suddenly, Helena wanted to run away from the creeping intimacy, the dangerous exploration that was sliding into their conversation, but she continued. "I always knew that I would be inadequate as a parent, but I knew that you would be a great dad."

"I did OK." He smiled.

It had taken years for Helena to get over Mark, and she wondered whether he pined for months or years for her, or had he found a random stranger to ease his pain. How long had it taken for him to get over her?

She had never really fallen in love with anyone except Mark, nor had she had such satisfying, exciting sex with anyone since. The memory of their lovemaking had haunted her all her life. Many times, she had wanted to contact him but had convinced herself that he would be furious, and never want to see her again.

Although she had gone to America with Graham Langton, she had soon realised what a terrible mistake she had made.

He had come to the college as a guest speaker, and was instantly attracted to the stunning Helena. By then, she was tired of struggling to buy a decent meal, slogging every evening in the coffee bar, and of the jumble sale clothes that she wore. She and Mark had had yet another disagreement about his busking, and she was bored.

It hadn't taken long to be flattered by Graham's attention, the expensive presents he bought her, his cars, the places he took her, and his ambition. But mainly, she was persuaded by his promises of an exciting job in New York.

She was also nearly three months' pregnant when she had left Mark. The last possible thing that she wanted or expected, and she knew that she had to get away before anyone, especially Mark, found out. She had no idea how it had happened, but it had, and she knew for certain, when her breasts had become tender and she had had no hint of a period for over two and a half months. Graham was the only person she had told and he offered an easy way out. He paid for her abortion, and she tried to put the whole incident out of her mind.

She had married Graham in Las Vegas after he had won $50,000 and generously given most of it to her. The marriage only lasted for ten months because Graham was not only a heavy drinker but a womaniser too. But, true to his word, he had bought her a beautiful new wardrobe, *and* been instrumental in getting her a job with a production company in New York. He had recognised not only her talent, but her ambition and drive.

She worked hard and was soon earning more money than she had ever thought possible. For Helena, it was her lifestyle and possessions that became important. For the first time in her life, she indulged in beautiful things that gave her pleasure: costly furniture and paintings, elegant jewellery, expensive perfume and fine champagne. She became Helena Langton-Cartwright, a well-admired and extremely professional director and producer working mainly in the New York theatre but then more often lately in films and television.

After divorcing Graham, she had been involved with a few testosterone-driven fuckwits, and one or two had managed to relieve her of money or possessions, so she had come to the conclusion that most men were bastards. Even so, she was never short of willing escorts; after all she was a good-looking woman, with an acerbic wit, and had developed an extensive knowledge of her craft. She was lonely at times, but always found that her money and status made up for the lack of a permanent partner. She adopted a cool, controlled hold on her emotional self, and all those years had avoided any relationship that took her outside her comfort zone.

In America, Helena had gained a great deal of respect and prestige but she had returned to England when she was in her mid forties, met and married Edward Hart. He was the director of a set design and building company, an old-fashioned engineer, who was at least twenty years her senior. He had never been married before and adored her. For Helena it was a comfortable arrangement, not the most satisfying, but Edward was a good-natured, undemanding man. She had respected and cared for him, but never felt the all-consuming passion that she had had for Mark. Edward had died in an accident only four years after they married, and she had been alone ever since.

"Tell me about the woman you are with," said Helena.

"Carol? She's lovely. We are getting married in the summer. I met her when my wife, Kate, was ill. She had a series of cancers that finally took her three years ago. Carol was a Macmillan nurse, who helped me care for Kate. I couldn't have coped without her."

"What would she think about us meeting up again, after all these years? Should we tell her?" Helena smiled teasingly.

Mark found himself wondering how Carol would react. *Badly,* he thought. "No. I'm asking you not to. In fact I am begging you not to." He smiled.

Helena was struck by the memory of his gentleness towards other people's feelings.

"I know it sounds silly, Helena, but Carol has somewhat of a jealous streak and in fact has found it difficult getting over that I was happily married before. I don't think she would like it at all. She is a good woman and I've been on my own a long time, and she's just what I need."

"What you need, rather than what you want?"

"Perhaps."

"Is that good enough for you now? It never used to be."

Careful, Helena thought. *You are treading on dangerous ground. Perhaps, he's really not given you a thought in all these years.*

She often recalled the wanton desire that had overtaken them whenever they touched each other. Every part, every crease and curve of each other's body had been explored, kissed, licked or stroked. In the shower, they had soaped and scrubbed, and laughed together. In bed, on the couch, or across the kitchen table, they made love, sometime playfully, sometimes passionately, and sometimes with a quiet intensity, gazing into each other's eyes. Nothing hidden or left out.

Watching him intently, she wondered if startling, sexy images of their naked bodies entwined, were running around inside his head too.

"A lot has happened since those days," Mark replied carefully.

Helena was having an unnerving effect on him. For the first time in years, his heart felt squeezed and excited. There was an awkward silence as he watched the ice in his gin and tonic melting. Lifting his eyes, he found she was smiling.

"I missed you so much when you left. This is really difficult, isn't it? Should I be telling you this now, after all these years?" he asked as he leaned toward her.

It's exactly what I want to hear, and I'll tell you how I feel too, thought Helena. *If I don't tell you now, the moment will pass, and perhaps you will never know how much I hated myself for being such a coward. How selfish I was. I can't tell you about the abortion though. That you would never forgive.*

"I know, I shouldn't have left you," she found herself saying. "Once I had gone, I couldn't come back. You *were* the love of my life and I've tried not to want you, not to think about you even, but it's like going on a diet; the minute you decide you will never eat another chocolate, you long for one. You can't wait until you have some, you fantasise about them." Helena laughed as the words tumbled out and she was surprised at herself. She was normally so controlled and rarely showed emotion. This was an element of herself that had been locked away since leaving Mark on that Sunday in July, when Graham had found her crying in the college garden. He was leaving the following morning and had invited her to go with him.

On reflection, she realised that her life would have been so entirely different, but would it have made up for the fabulous career and success she had enjoyed, and the extraordinarily good life she had had? *No, not really.* She shuddered as a mental image of herself with a family, lugging groceries home, attending school plays, and dealing with the endless traumas that children brought.

Mark laughed, then said quietly ,"I have spent a lifetime hoping that we would meet again."

Helena's eyes filled with tears. Even when she lost Edward, tears had not come to the surface, and here she was, only an hour with Mark, and he had stirred something that had lain dormant for years.

Mark carefully took her hand, and as she tightened her grip, it renewed the deep longing he had for her. "You too, I can see it in your eyes. But it's the wrong time for us now. I can't let Carol down. She has been such a rock for me."

Helena was thinking just the opposite. *Really? It couldn't be a better time. Perhaps now is exactly the right time. A better time for us both. We are both free and available. Except for Carol... bloody Carol. I won't let her stand between us. You obviously don't love her... Perhaps if we spent the night together.*

As Mark was preparing to leave, Helena found herself saying, 'Goodnight. Can we meet again soon?'

"It's already midnight, and Carol will be concerned."

"Tomorrow then?"

"Tomorrow evening would be good. Carol wants to see the crooner again, but I said I would like to go to the casino. Will you meet me there at eight-thirty, and we can spend a bit more time together before we get to Barbados?"

Helena suppressed the notion of delaying him so that Carol would be suspicious. After all, there were still two days before they reached the islands, and Helena was a determined woman once she set her sights on something. Perhaps by then, Mark would see that this was fate playing a hand for them to be together at last.

The following evening confirmed Helena's belief that their meeting again after so long was definitely 'fate' taking a hand, and that Carol would have to see that she and Mark should be together.

"Come to my cabin," Helena whispered, "Carol need not know." Helena had assured herself that renewing their passion would convince him.

"No, I couldn't," he replied but Helena had already taken his hand to lead him away. Helena had a large cabin with a balcony, and a bottle of champagne on ice waiting for them.

Being with Helena was everything that Mark remembered, even her lovely, exotic perfume had moved up market, but still it brought back the sweetness of the memories. Her body, long-forgotten, had become instantly familiar from the moment they started to make love, and although the speed and agility of their youth had slowed to a more deliciously, romantic pace, it was still as exciting and passionate as it had been all those years before. Mark was surprised how they easily slipped back into knowing what pleased and excited each other. They were heady and dreamy with the love-making and champagne, when they realised how long they had been together. Helena stretched her long brown arm around him to delay him even more when he said, "Oh Helena, what have we done? This will break Carol's heart."

"Don't worry, Mark, she will get used to it."

Helena's reply did worry Mark. It was said with such confidence and broached no chance that this might not continue, whilst he could only worry about how Carol would react if she found out. She was quite a volatile woman and Mark was in no mood for conflict. Guilty as he felt, he thought he had to find a way to stop Carol finding out and wracked his brain for an acceptable explanation.

"Do you want to tell me what's going on?" Carol asked when Mark finally turned up. It was over two hours since the show had finished and she had been waiting in the bar next to the casino.

"I can't explain here," Mark said, casting a furtive glance around the bar.

People were coming out of the late show, and settling down for a drink before retiring. He had no intention of explaining anything to Carol in front of a crowd. How could he explain anyway? It was such an unexpected discovery, and he was confused by his reaction. "We need to talk... I need to explain. Come out on deck and... "

Mark took Carol's arm and led her through the doors and up the stairs to a higher deck where there were fewer people.

There was quite a wind blowing up, but Carol marched ahead. They reached the massive tent used for golf practice before she turned so that she could look at him. She leant on the railings, her back to the sea, as she said quietly. "So... explain then. Why were you so late? Where have you been? I've sat in that bar on my own for over two hours, No, that's not quite true, I did go to the cabin once to see if you'd forgotten our plans... but no, no sign of you there. I don't like being left on my own." She sniffed, her eyes dark with anger as she stood waiting for his response.

"Have you drunk too much? Have you gambled all our money away...? Why are you looking like that?"

Mark couldn't answer, his mind swirling with thoughts of Helena. Should he lie? Should he try to explain that his burning desire for Helena had wiped out all rational thought? How could he tell Carol that? She simply wouldn't understand. How could he even begin to explain?

"No. I erm... I've... No... Hell I..." But before he could form a sentence, a movement from behind caught his attention, and he gasped as Helena stepped calmly out of the shadows and answered for him.

"He's been with me." It was said lightly and smiling she walked forward, her hand extended towards Carol as she continued confidently. "Helena Langton-Cartwright. Mark and I are old friends, aren't we, darling? Very old friends. Very good friends," and without hesitating continued as Mark gulped and Carol gaped, "You must be Carol, the nurse. Mark has been

41

telling me how invaluable you have been to him. So nice to meet you. We've had a lovely time catching up, haven't we darling?"

Carol's eyes darted from Mark to Helena then back again, and ignoring Helena's outstretched hand, gasped in outrage, her anger rising in her throat. She understood instantly and no explanation from Mark could have made it any clearer. Helena was making sure of that. Eyes narrowed and teeth clenched, she turned on Mark. "Really... So *are* you going to explain? What *exactly* does she mean. Old friends... good friends?"

Not moving or speaking, Mark stood rigid, so Carol turned back to Helena, her voice rising another pitch. "You do know we are engaged? He did tell you, I assume."

Helena moved forward, gripped the rail, turned and perched herself next to Carol so that she too, was facing Mark.

"Oh, yes of course he told me, Carol. He told me all about you and how wonderful you have been and how grateful he is." She smiled at Mark who was shaking his head and had retreated so far back that he was almost leaning against the wall of the ship.

Incensed by Helena's cool manner, Carol dropped her evening bag and scarf and hurled herself across the deck towards Mark with fists raised. "You bastard. While I've been waiting for you, you've been having sex with her, haven't you? Your old friend... your good friend. We're engaged. Doesn't that mean anything to you?"

The wind was by now whipping up Carol's chiffon dress, showing her large cellulite-ridden thighs but she was intent on striking Mark, and ignored the fact that her underwear was at the point of being exposed.

Raising his arms to avoid the blows, Mark tried to defend himself. "Carol please… of course it means something to me, but Helena and I… we were in love. It was a long time ago."

"Tonight's not a long time ago." Carol screeched as she flew at him again, raining blows onto his arms and chest. One blow landed squarely on his chin so that he staggered backward, and would have fallen if the wall had not been behind him.

The wind had risen so that even the raised voices could only be heard at close quarters and there was nobody else on deck.

"And you," spat Carol as she turned to face Helena. "How could you? He is my fiancé. He loves me."

The ship rolled gently. The sky had blackened and the deck lights were flickering so it was not easy to see the next turn of events, but Helena lifted her voice. "I don't think so. He's been with me all evening, drinking champagne, and having a wonderful time. I doubt if he thought of you even once." All the while Helena looked totally relaxed, even though she was holding tightly to the rail.

"Carol, don't." Mark leaped forward but the wind muffled his words and before he had a chance to stop her, she lurched forward toward Helena. At that moment, a great peal of thunder and lightening struck with such force that the deck lights went off and the wind rose to a mighty whoosh, gathering Carol's dress and lifting it up, up and over her face in a tangled mess. On reaching the rail, the momentum of her rush towards Helena did not stop, and Carol hit the rail and tipped forward, her legs

43

lifting into the air. Helena had stepped to one side still grasping the rail, and Mark watched in horror as Carol flipped over both the rail and the safety rope.

In a calm sea, she would have hit the lower deck and probably suffered a few broken bones but the great liner had lurched so suddenly that Carol floated straight over the side, past all the lower decks, and disappeared almost instantly into the heaving, black waves below.

Helena's screaming eventually brought the safety team out on deck, but as the minutes passed by, it was obvious that Carol had disappeared into the depths forever.

As the Captain later explained, even though a thorough search was always made, at night, in the middle of the ocean, it was unlikely anyone could survive for more than a few minutes especially, if the weather was as bad as it was that night.

Statements were taken and as strangers, Mark and Helena explained the events to the Head of Security, who took meticulous details of the position of each of them when the 'incident' took place. Due to the fact that the golf tent had obscured the CCT cameras and the lights had gone out, there was nothing and nobody else to substantiate the evidence or to suggest it was anything but an unfortunate accident.

Mark was in such a state of shock, recalling only that the ship had lurched unexpectedly and Carol's dress had lifted with the suddenness of the high winds, and she had lost her sense of direction.

Helena calmly told how the rolling ship had caused her to feel slightly nauseous so she had wandered onto deck for some fresh air, and seen Mark and Carol.

No, she had never set eyes on Carol Wilkinson before that night and yes, she had only been there a moment or two when she saw Carol fall over the rail.

"Her dress blew up over her face," Helena had explained, "and I suppose she didn't realise that she was so close to the railings. Yes, a terrible accident, could have happened to anyone."

So accepting the word of the two passengers at the scene, he wrote his notes for his report saying, 'We take safety on board very seriously but we have no immediate help available in the open sea.'

Seeing Mark's stricken face, he added, 'The nearest port authority is too far away but I *will* ask immediately for a search to be made, but I must tell you that there is little hope I am afraid.'

Still in a deep state of shock, Mark arranged to be transferred by helicopter to Barbados from where he would fly back to the UK. Carol had a large family who would need an explanation. An accident, a tragic accident.

Helena was resigned to Mark leaving. "Of course you must go, darling. They will need you," she told him with a sigh and a loving hug as they said farewell, knowing that it would be only a matter of time before they would be together again and that there would be no recriminations, no accusations, no evidence of any misconduct.

Fate definitely, fate indeed, thought Helena with a smile as Mark waved a sad goodbye. *Yes, I still am the same selfish bitch I always was, but finally I will have my lover back where he belongs.*

Suppressing a giggle, she thought, *No one need*

ever know about having my foot ever so slightly extended at just the precise moment that Carol had tripped forward.

***

ANNABELLE – Chocolate Dream

One of the first things Annabelle noticed was how incredibly friendly the crew and staff were. Smiling, nodding and courteous; the Indian waiters, Philippine waitresses and the assorted crew made everyone feel special and welcomed.

Annabelle had never been on a cruise before and certainly never attempted to have a holiday on her own. Her friends had assured her that it was the best way to find new friends. 'You'll never be alone,' Trevor, her mate from the poetry and writing group had assured her.

It was true, and so far, Annabelle had never felt lonely or at a loss for anything to do. There were so many organised activities that you could fill the whole day if you wanted to. She had already met Angela, determined that no one should be lonely or left out. So far she had attended dance classes, lectures, talks, painting class, theatre and musical productions, avoided the sports lounge, the bridge players and the many quiz games, but on the whole had a very good time.

Every evening she had dined with different people, sometimes the single group organised by Angela, sometimes on the random seating where she met mainly friendly sorts with varying accents and interests. She had been served by several different waiters all of whom smiled and flirted companionably with the ladies and were courteous and helpful with everyone.

Black tie evenings meant all the ladies could bring out their best sparklers and ball-gowns, and shine, even though most of the holiday-makers were mainly retired and at least some of them had been so for twenty years or more. Regardless of hearing aids, dinner-lady arms and walnut whip faces, the ladies shone as never before, as the gentlemen sweated in their dinner jackets and bow ties.

Amongst the single ladies, there were a few gentlemen who spread themselves around as best they could and even managed to flirt with the plethora of widows who were busy spending the children's inheritance.

Today, Annabelle had taken a break from all the activities and settled herself away from the pool and the brilliant Caribbean sun and opened the latest Kate Atkinson that she hadn't yet had a chance to start.

The cruise had been a great idea and after the previous two years of operations and chemotherapy, it was proving to be just what she needed. On top of the breast cancer and surgery, Annabelle was getting used to being on her own again as her husband James had died unexpectedly of a heart attack last year.

"Good morning Mrs Gregory." A silky voice interrupted her thoughts. "How are you today?"

Squinting slightly in the bright morning sunshine Annabelle lifted her eyes. One of the handsome dark-skinned Goan waiters stood before her. He was intensely good-looking with shiny white teeth and flashing dark eyes. His badge identified him as Luis.

"Oh, lovely thank you," she replied, thinking perhaps he was going to ask if she wanted a drink. How did he remember her name though? There were nearly two thousand people on this ship. He was smiling at her. Did he have a message for her?

A moment of panic.

But, no surely it wouldn't be a waiter sent to give

her message from home and nobody else that she had met on board would be sending her messages.

She waited.

"I have seen you and I smiled at you at breakfast this morning."

"Yes."

"I am not following you, but I have been looking for you. I wanted so much to speak to you."

"Oh, why?"

"Because you are beautiful and you smile at everyone."

He's flirting with me, thought Annabelle so she asked, "Are you flirting with me?" at the same time trying to judge his age. Younger than her eldest son who was forty-two that year, that was for sure.

"Do you think so?" he replied. "I have seen you and I wanted to tell you I liked you, so I thought..."

"What?"

"That I would come and say 'Hello'."

"Oh, so you are flirting with me then?"

"Am I?" he replied, beginning to look worried that Annabelle was not responding as he expected.

"How old are you?"

He grinned again, showing his white teeth.

"You know I am old enough to be your mother," she said quietly.

"I like older women."

"Oh."

"Especially those who look like you. I have watched you every day. You are perfect. You can not be more than fifty-eight or nine."

Bloody hell, thought Annabelle, feeling momentarily flattered that this tall, good-looking young man should be making overtures to her.

"Ah well… " She hesitated.

"Is that a no then?

"No, what?"

"You know, I could come to your cabin," he twinkled.

"I am very flattered but I think it must be... "

"Is it because I am a waiter or the colour of my skin?"

Oh no, she wanted to say, *you are absolutely delicious, but I am seventy, even though I might not look quite that old. I certainly would feel it next to your beautiful chocolate body. It's a long time since mine was exposed to anything more radical than the communal showers at the spa where I have my monthly massage.*

Annabelle smiled and even though she knew that this boy was far from home, lonely for a woman, an opportunist who probably had a wife and six children in Goa, she felt extremely flattered to be called beautiful, and perfect, and fifty-nine. Hey ho, thank God for all the vitamins she had been taking. She glowed inwardly and silently thanked him for lifting her flagging confidence from zero to one hundred in a matter of moments. She felt compelled to inquire. "Do you have much success? You know with the older ladies… One does hear that... There are those who..."

"Yes, sometimes," he answered. He knew by now that Annabelle was not going to be tempted by his beautiful smile and the promise of a fantasy romp with a brown skinned Lothario. "In five years I suppose about twenty times, but do not tell anyone. And do not repeat this conversation, please."

"No, no of course not. Why would I?" Annabelle

replied knowing full well that every syllable would be repeated word-for-word in the book of short stories that she was writing about cruising.

***

ROGER – What Goes Around

Roger Trenton-Keating smiled across the table at his wife Jessica, who was laughing with an extremely large, sweaty gentleman, whose stomach seemed at the point of bursting through his, obviously new, frilly shirt. The black tie evenings on the ship necessitated every man be suitably dressed in dinner jacket, and bow tie, even though it was glaringly obvious that it was far too warm for such attire, once the ship reached the waters of the Caribbean. The said gentleman, was mopping his brow with his napkin as he listened to Jessica's story about the last holiday they had had together, four years ago in Lisbon, in the wettest week of the entire year.

It was so nice to see her laughing and happy again. Roger thought. The last few years had been difficult for both of them, but particularly for her. The cruise in the Caribbean was his attempt to get their life, and their marriage, back together again.

Jessica looked radiant this evening in her scarlet chiffon, her skin glowed from their wonderful sunshine-filled days on the beaches of all the islands they had visited so far. Her body looked toned and fit from all the walking, swimming and the daily on-board Yoga classes. Her hair was newly cut, and set in a soft bob. She smiled at him across the table.

Roger was feeling thoroughly pleased with himself that he had managed to talk Jessica into this last-ditch attempt to reconcile their marriage.

They had made love, hesitatingly at first, and then with renewed energy and passion, as they recalled their early years together. He had carefully planned everything, from the red roses and champagne to the special bookings in the spa. The best suite with a balcony, and no expense spared.

Dessert was being served, and Roger, having decided on the lemon meringue pie, lifted his eyes to survey the room. It was enormous, and over two thousand people on the ship dined there at varying times of the evening.

On the table behind him, they were discussing the rumour that someone had gone overboard a couple of nights before when the storms were raging. What other reason could there be for the helicopter circling, and then landing on the ship?

At the next table, a petite, blonde lady of indiscernible age was explaining that she used to be a dancer, and that was why she ate like a sparrow.

"Habits of a lifetime rarely change when we retire," she said. "I think my stomach shrunk when I was about eighteen, and I have been as thin as a post ever since. "Had to be. Couldn't work otherwise, darlings."

Roger smiled inwardly at the conversation.

The voice that replied pinged into his consciousness with alarm bells ringing. With terrifying clarity, he recognised Gabriella's husky voice.

"Same in television, sweetie. Got to look like a pipe-cleaner, or you're out before you can say Jamie Oliver. Even he's had to lose weight to stay on, you know."

Leaning slightly forward, Roger could see Gabriella's smooth suntanned shoulder, and her arm with the sparkling diamond-encrusted gold bracelet he had given her just the month before. Panic rippled through his body, and his breath clogged in his throat, as he remembered the occasion. It was their final weekend together. They were in Paris for a filming of the last of the series of 'Reminiscent Fashion of the Century' that Roger had been directing for BBC2. In her role as a fashionable and mature presenter, Gabriella had been instrumental in organising their time together, on and off the show.

He had, in fact, tired of Gabriella over a year before, but he and Jessica were by then leading almost separate lives, and she was talking of leaving and moving into town, ostensibly, to be close to their daughter Poppy. However, it was their son Christopher, who had informed his father how desperately unhappy Jessica was, *and* that she knew about, but never mentioned his affair with Gabriella.

"Put it right before it's too late, Dad. Mum loves you so much, she won't ever publicly disgrace you. You are both close to retiring, and she doesn't really want to be on her own."

Roger had given it a lot of thought. He and Jessica *had* been together for over thirty years and he knew that he loved her, and she loved him. He decided it was time to make amends.

He had tried to explain to Gabriella that their affair couldn't go on, but nothing he said quite convinced her. She had cried when Roger had finally told her, that their three-year relationship had to end. To salve his conscience, he had told her that Jessica was desperately ill, and needed him with her and although he adored her, Gabriella, it was his duty to stay with his wife. Lying had never been that difficult for Roger. The story had rolled off his tongue and he looked suitably saddened. The bracelet was a parting gift, inscribed with their names, and the message, 'Forever in my heart'.

He now watched as the bracelet moved up and down her arm as she spoke. That was all he could see from where he sat.

He hadn't told Gabriella that he was bringing Jessica away on a cruise to try to save his marriage. She obviously, had not told him her plans either.

The eight people at the next table, including Gabriella, rose and filed out of the dining room without turning in the direction of Roger and Jessica's table. How he had missed seeing her before, he didn't know, after all they had been at sea over a week. But that was the nature of these big cruises and with so many people aboard, every evening you met new faces. What would happen, if she saw him with the obviously very healthy Jessica?

Jessica stopped laughing, when she looked across the table and saw his stricken face. He had tried to rise but stopped as his chair hit the floor behind him.

"Darling, what's the matter? Are you ill?"

Roger couldn't speak. The pain started in his chest, moved down his arm, and exploded through his body in an instant.

"Wonder what happened to that one?" asked the diminutive blonde, as she and Gabriella watched the coffin being taken off the ship in Barbados to be flown home the next morning.

***

PAM & TONY – Animal Rights

Pam sipped her cappuccino, reflecting on the previous evening spent with the handsome, and totally outrageous, Daniel Mr-Gorgeous-Crooner Morreneo, one of the ships many entertainers. A small smile played across her lips as she recalled the fun evening they had spent together. He had freely admitted that he liked his life on board ship as it gave him easy and instant access to as many woman as he could handle. Nothing had actually happened between them as he was definitely *not* what she was looking for. She was looking for a much bigger fish, and he was only a moderately successful singer. By his own admission, he spent most of his money on alcohol and having fun. She had confided in him exactly why she was spending her last few bob on this expensive cruise, so he too had been more than frank with her about his motivations.

"I am not being braggie," he had told her, "but I could bed a babe after every gig if I wanted to. The women in my audience are pushovers. Don't present much of a challenge really. Always have a few groupies who pretend they are sleeping with Frank Sinatra, Matt Monroe, or whoever I happen to be doing on that night. Hum them a few lines and they are putty in my hands. Same on the cruises, although one or two are vergin' on being coffin dodgers. Anyway, got to rush."

Pam had laughed, as he winked and set off toward the casino, thinking to herself how ridiculous some women were to be taken in by such an obvious rogue.

Suddenly a familiar voice interrupted her thoughts.

"Pammy? I knew it was you. Bloody 'ell, I haven't

seen you for ages. Wot you doin' 'ere?" yelled Sharon, as she sashayed toward the deck five Costa coffee shop. She was wearing a pea green tea-shirt with a purple **'I'm going to Barbados'** emblazoned across the front.

Pam's smile turned to shocked disbelief when she saw Sharon approaching. "Oh my God, Sharon ... shush, shush. Why did you have to be on this bloody ship. Don't look round... and... don't call me Pammy. This holiday, I am Paloma here." Pam answered in a whisper.

"Paloma? Well, I have got to say you look more like a Paloma than a Pammy. Give us a clue then?" Sharon said, eyeing the expensive, floaty sundress and the high-heel sandals Pam was sporting.

Mind you, she always looked good. Had the sort of figure that would look great in a paper bag. Lovely hair too, a real deep chestnut and glossy as a conker, thought Sharon, *I was always a bit envious, especially when she married Steven.*

Pam knew Sharon well enough to know that she would want to know exactly what was going on. She was an old friend, and as honest and straightforward as anybody you could ever meet. They had worked together, briefly, at Denton's in the nineties and had had many a night out after Pam had divorced Joe. She was wise and trustworthy. In fact Sharon was the first person that Pam had told when she had met Steven, and confided her intention of marrying him, purely for the lifestyle he could provide for her. She hadn't seen Sharon for over a year, as they lived further apart since Pam had married Steven. They just met randomly, from time to time, and had a quick lunch or coffee, depending on the circumstances.

"Don't ask. But yeah, I'm on a mission. I need to find a husband."

Sharon lifted her eyebrows in confusion. 'usband? What happened to Mr Successful-Rich-Wanker-Banker, Steven?

"Dead."

"No? You've only been married five years."

"Yep, but the bloody dick-head fell off the roof and killed himself."

"What was 'e doin' on the roof?"

"How the hell should I know? He never told me what he was doing... trying to fly perhaps? God knows... Perhaps he was adjusting the 'thingy' dish that's supposed to send six hundred channels into my living room. Anyway, listen Sharon, I'm in a mess I can tell you... but, please pretend we've just met *and* call me Paloma."

Sharon looked intrigued. Pam knew there was nothing she liked better than a bit of a mystery. "Right-ho, will do." With a wink, she turned, and pulled up a bar stool.

Pam decided it was probably best to enlighten her before she gave the game away.

"Right. Just keep mum... Anyway, what the devil are you doin' here?" she asked. "I wouldn't have thought —?"

"I'm with me mum. Big win on the Bingo, an' she says, 'Right, then girl, where do you want to go?' an' I says, 'Caribbean' an' she says, 'Right-ho', an' 'ere we are."

"Bloody hell! Your mother's here too!" Pam exclaimed, recalling Sharon's diminutive mother, a seventy-year-old Hattie who smoked like a chimney, and had a laugh like a farting buffalo.

"She won't say nothing, if I tell her. She'll think it's a right lark."

"Warn her then."

"So... what are you doing 'ere. Are you really looking for a new 'usband Pammy... Paloma." Sharon grinned.

"Exactly."

"What, exactly?" Sharon asked, as she settled back onto the bar stool.

"A six foot gorgeous millionaire who adores me, hangs on my every word, and wants to look after me for the rest of my life... What do you think I'm looking for? I don't care if he's a bald, bloody midget as long as I can keep my house, my horses and my account at Selfridges. I had to sell the Merc to come on this cruise."

"What about the Wanker-Banker's money?"

"Left every penny to his ex and his daughter. Not a bloody farthing to me... can't even pay the mortgage, never mind the bills." Pam sighed dramatically.

"Oh, poor you. I'll keep me eyes open then. I've got to go. I'll tell my mum… she'll be tickled pink. See you later. Good hunting… Paloma," Sharon winked.

As she hurried off to meet her mum, Daniel Mr-Gorgeous-Crooner came down the stairway. His deeply suntanned face beamed as people recognised him, and he lifted his immaculately manicured finger-tips to wave at several of the old couples sitting around.

"Mr Popular," smiled Pam as he approached the coffee bar and perched himself on a stool beside her.

"Got to keep the punters happy."

"You obviously are," Pam said, watching the

60

women admiring him. "And where did you get to last night?"

"What do you think eh." He winked. A glass of wine appeared before him, and the waiter indicated a beautifully dressed, slim matron, of perhaps retirement age, sitting across the atrium. "Ahem, excuse me," he said as he slipped off the stool and strode toward the waiting wine-provider.

"Good luck."

Finishing her coffee, Pam decided a prowl around the upper deck again, just to see if any of the single gentlemen were increasing their tans, or perhaps needed someone to rub on their suntan lotion! Some hope. It was already day eight of the month-long cruise and she had not found a single possible candidate.

She knew she looked good, in her pale floaty sundress, but she should probably change her shoes. It wouldn't do to keel over at the wrong moment.

Half an hour later, Pam was sitting at the bar on the top deck under a giant orange umbrella, sipping a soda water. Her feet were now prettily encased in soft beige leather sandals, borrowed from Janice, her neighbour.

No likely candidates up there either, unless you counted the short, soft bodied, fifty-plus-year-old who was settling his ancient mother onto a recliner. *Gay, I would guess, and probably waiting for her to keel over,* Pam thought. *Still, anything is possible.*

He headed toward the bar so Pam got a better look at him. *Still got a bit of hair and with a good suit might look presentable.* She gave him a radiant smile as he passed by, leaving him in no doubt that it was him she was smiling at. He puffed up like a pouter-pigeon.

Perhaps not gay then.

Nevertheless, he trotted back to his mother without a second look at Pam so she decided to take a walk. She had wandered the whole top deck, and swimming pool area, and not seen another interesting man, so she was feeling pretty frustrated. Although she considered herself to be strong and independent, tough some would say, she had never managed to be financially secure without the help of a man. Being strong meant being cool and in control, holding back from any deep involvement and keeping feelings safe and peripheral. Growing up in a household where she had felt alien and unloved, Pam learned early on how to be detached. She was not looking for love, only a big bank account to solve her problems.

Oh well, she mused, *perhaps I'll meet some rich yacht owner on one of the islands. Otherwise I'll be in shit creek.*

Pam had less than a hundred pounds in her bank account and the Wanker-Banker's family were already in the house, waiting for instructions about Blaze and Trixie, her beloved horses, who were under threat of being sent off for sale if she didn't take them away within the next month. Even if she could get a job, it was unlikely that it would afford the keep two highly-bred horses, and then there were her dogs, of course. She would have to find somewhere, soon. Perhaps she would have to sell the horses, but her animals were the only loves in her life. She opened her bag, and sifted through the bundle of bills, receipts, old lottery tickets and photographs. She found one of her beloved dogs, Butch, her German shepherd and Didi, her beautiful borzoi, both still in the house with her grasping stepdaughter, and her mother.

They had promised to care for the dogs and horses for three months only. Pam knew that of all the things she could give up, her animals were not one of them. Gazing lovingly at the photograph strengthened her resolve to find a rich man.

"Lovely, aren't they?" said a voice beside her.

Lifting her eyes, she found herself looking into a pair of dark, hazel ones, topped by an unruly mop of dark red hair. A lopsided smile gave the owner a rakish look, and although he was tall, was leaning forward, to gaze over her shoulders at her photograph.

"What?" she asked, turning to take a better look.

"Are they yours?" he gushed.

Pam took a long hard look at him. Where had he appeared from? Not bad, though, dressed in a long sleeved shirt and creased chinos. A bit old fashioned perhaps, but probably the best-looking bloke on board, except for Mr Morreneo.

"Sorry, but I do love dogs. I'm Anthony Forster-Brown." He pushed a tanned hand toward her. "Have you cruised before?"

"No, you?"

"Once, around the Med. Many years ago. Have been too busy lately... business you know."

"What sort of business?

"Finance, properties, investments, all sorts."

A swift glow of interest crossed Pam's mind.

"Oh, me too. I have an investment I'm trying to hang on to at the moment. Just need the right help."

"Really I'm looking for a partner as well... a business partner."

Pam smiled coyly at him. "Are you on your own... on the cruise?"

"Yes all alone. I saw you with your friend earlier."

"Oh, er no, not a friend really, an acquaintance. I'm Paloma Wright-Morgan by the way." He took her hand again, quite unnecessarily, and squeezed it gently.

"Very pleased to meet you Mrs... Ms Wright-Morgan?

"Call me Paloma. So, what exactly is it that you do, Anthony?"

"Work in the city, you know."

"No, I don't know. Bit vague. What exactly?"

"Stocks and shares, and things."

Yer right, thought Pam, knowing a storyteller when she saw one. *Who did he think he was kidding?* "How are you doing then?" she asked, taking another good look at his clothes and especially at his work-hardened hands.

"Ah, well, business is slow at the moment. I have my eye on some property investment. Just have to raise the capital."

"Where?"

"Where? Err... actually all over, you know."

"No, I don't know. Tell me." She turned to him, raising an eyebrow. He wasn't a very good liar and she knew only too well, being a past master herself.

"Well?" She tapped him on the chest. "Don't kid a kidder. I was married to a banker. Tell me what you really do."

At that moment, Pam saw Sharon and her mother approaching, and Sharon having seen her, lapsed into a giggling avoidance manoeuvre and moved across toward the recliners on the side deck.

Anthony noticed. "Oh, that's your friend, isn't it."

"Hi darlings, see you later," said Pam in her poshest accent, at the same time lifting her finger in a

64

dismissive wave. She was hoping Sharon wouldn't approach. She wanted to know more about Mr Forster-Brown.

"Right now. The truth?"

"I'm... I am a banker. In the city you know... mostly, but sometimes not." He hesitated as Pam raised a enquiring eyebrow.

"Well... No, I'm not really. A failed one, actually. No, not even that. How come you sussed me so fast?" Anthony whispered, looking somewhat embarrassed.

"Look at your cuffs, for God's sake. No investment banker would be seen dead with frayed cuffs like that. And your hands are as rough as a bin man's. Every banker that *I* have ever met has been immaculate. You're obviously up to no good, Anthony... or is it perhaps, not Anthony?"

"It's Tony, plain Tony Smith, and you?" He grinned.

"I told you, Paloma Wright-Morgan." She smiled. He had come clean so what was the point in trying to kid him? "OK, it's Pam Wright."

They moved off together, towards a quiet seat at the back of the upper deck, and Tony went to the bar and ordered the cocktail of the day. Pam watched the sunshine skimming across the waves as the ship moved onward and thought, *Just my luck, the only good-looking blokes on board; one a second rate, crooning Lothario looking for a good time, and this animal-loving pauper. He's probably on the same mission as me. Hell's teeth, what am I going to do? No bloody good to me. I've lost interest already. The last thing I need is a poor man.*

She waved to Mr and Mrs Frensham as they walked by. She had met them several days before, and was working on an invite to their country house in Dorset. They had an unmarried son, who sounded quite hideous, but would inherit the family fortune.

Going by the huge diamonds, emeralds and gold they both displayed, especially on black-tie nights, it was probably quite extensive. Mrs Frensham looked like an extravagant Christmas tree, and Mr Frensham advertised their wealth with his huge Rolex, gold rings and chains. On his fat, sausagey middle finger, he wore a ring with a diamond that must have cost, at least, the price of a small house.

"Just look at the thousands of pounds walking around on that pair." Pam laughed gaily as Tony returned to the table with their drinks. "They must be worth a fortune. Would pay a few of my bills, that's for sure."

Tony watched the Frenshams. "And mine," he said finally. "Do you think they would miss them if I relieved them of those filthy jewels?"

Instantly Pam's interest was renewed and she turned back toward him. "Hey, are you a thief... a professional? So come on, tell me. Is that what you're doing on this cruise? I knew it, you're after the same as me. In a predicament are you? How can you afford a cruise?"

"Actually, I have a very kind, wealthy godfather. The cruise was a present from him. He thought I should take a break, as I have been working so hard, so I thought I might do the Caribbean."

"Yeah, right. Real reason?"

"Can you keep a secret, lovely Pam Wright? Let's get another drink then perhaps, I will tell you. Can I trust you?" His hazel eyes twinkled.

"Of course."

"Let's get to know each other first. Will you accompany me on shore to Barbados tomorrow?"

Pam thought that it was a wonderful idea but she didn't want anyone cramping her style, and intended to continue to looking for some way out of her predicament, even if it was only a temporary one.

"Actually, I am meeting some friends at the yacht club. In town... they are old neighbours of mine. I would invite you too but... well no, I can't. It wouldn't look right... having recently lost my husband, you know. Even though he was a total wanker, they were rather fond of him."

Tony laughed loudly. "In that case we will meet up when we set sail again."

On arrival at Barbados, Pam disembarked, looking sleek and elegant in white capri pants and a lime-green soft silk shirt under which she had the skimpiest white bikini which she intended to show off at the impressive and very expensive yacht club in St Michael's Bay. Arriving in a hired limousine and knowing that they were busy preparing for the following month's regatta, she gained entrance on the pretext that she was a visiting journalist.

She loved the happy atmosphere, the colours and the fabulous yachts, some of them up to twenty metres long. She ordered a Pina colada and gazed at the comings and goings of the very rich who moored their boats in that fabulous setting. Many of the larger ones she knew would be chartered, but the cost was enormous and anyone who could afford them had a few 'bob'. The biggest had hunky tanned crews, but she wasn't interested in them. Been there, done that. Now was the time to consider the future, she needed to meet the owners. Time was short but nothing was going her way. She walked and chatted, trying to find rich owners. Suntanned and bejewelled ladies sat on the terrace or lay on the shiny decks whilst locals served them with exotic canapés and cocktails. Available rich, free men were just not to be found.

Panic set in as the day wore on. *Oh, I want so much to have that lifestyle, to be in that position again.* Pam thought as a few salty tears escaped and ran down her cheeks. *Actually, no, what I really want is my pets in a place where I can care for them and love them without thinking about how much they cost.*

She returned, disappointed to the cruise ship earlier than she expected, having spent the best of a day pretty much on her own, and despite her best efforts, didn't meet a single eligible male.

Tony was in the bar when Pam emerged, dressed for dinner. She looked stunning and knew it, in a pearly-green, soft silk figure-hugging dress. Despite her better judgement, she was very pleased to see him. He looked quite a dish that evening, even though his shirt was slightly crumpled, his dinner suit obviously borrowed and well worn and didn't fit him quite perfectly, he was scrubbed shiny and his hair neatly combed.

"Have you had a good day, lovely Paloma?"

"Yes, stunning, thank you." She wasn't going to tell him that she had spent it alone. "And you, what have you been up to?"

"Went to a quiet beach and thought about you."

"Did you now and… what were your thoughts?"

"Want to get to know you better, that's all. I think we probably have a lot in common."

Pam grinned and answered quietly. "Oh, quite probably. More than we both know, I suspect. Are you going to tell me what you are doing on this cruise all alone?"

"Yes."

"Are you looking for a rich widow?"

"Not really, although it might have been a possibility, till I met you."

"Really." Pam watched him carefully to see if he was speaking sincerely. Perhaps he thought she had money, after all she was expensively dressed and it wasn't cheap doing this sort of holiday on your own. She was good at reading people; he was looking straight into her eyes and there wasn't a hint of deceit. In a way, she felt sorry now that she had lied to him about Barbados.

"I mean it," he said. "Yes, I need money as I have some horrible debts to pay off, mainly incurred by my scurrilous ex business partner, but some of my own making. Having met you… I want to be straight with you… I really like you. I will find a way to sort my money problems… somehow."

"Legally or illegally?"

He shrugged and smiled at her, took her hand and led her into dinner.

Several hours later, having had a good bottle of wine, a lovely meal and at least two after dinner liqueurs, they sat on the moonlit deck, watching the stars. Both felt relaxed and comfortable with each other and had put their considerations to one side. Tony was easy to talk to so, when he asked her to tell him more about herself, she felt no embarrassment. "You really want to know? We were dirt poor, lived in Leeds, never knew who my father was. When I was seventeen, I hadn't got a decent grade, didn't know what I wanted to do. My mother kept telling me I would amount to nothing, and I believed her. She only ever had time for my brothers, because they earned money and tried to look after us. I was considered useless, and she told me to piss off so many times that in the end, I did. I went traveling. I only had about thirty quid, and took off, on what I thought would be a big adventure. I wanted to meet different people, you know... When you've been brought up in a small town, the world is inviting. Not really, though, not if you've got no dosh. I didn't get far, got a job in Paris, for a couple of months, and lived in a grotty hostel. Saved enough to get down to the south, and camped in Cavaliere with a group of hippies. I got a job there, in a posh kennels. Mucking out mainly. Run by a couple, Anton and Rosie Bencario, who had been in the circus, so they taught me how to tightrope and trapeze."

Tony was interested and raised his eyebrow. "You can tightrope? I am impressed, I hate heights."

"I loved it and got really good at it, and did a few seaside shows."

"Really, what happened then?"

"I got tired of the shit, the cat and dog shit, you know, so I got on a train to Barcelona. Met this gorgeous lezzie there, called Luisa. She was a singer. Thought I might try it for a bit... you know... the lezzie bit, but then I met her twin brother Paulo, who looked just like her, but with a dick, so I moved in with him." Pam grinned and wiped her finger across her cheeks. "Are you

70

shocked, Tony?" she asked.

"No, we've all done things that we would rather forget. Go on."

"Stayed with him for six months, and then came home, well, not home really, Watford actually, never went back to Leeds. Worked in Boots, Bhs, McDonald's and Costa coffee, all dead end jobs, got the sack, and married stupid Joe, who worked in the print works. Bit desperate, really, 'cos I didn't really love him, but he had a good job. Joe buggered off after six months. I wasn't sorry. I eventually convinced the local estate agent to give me a job. There was this big new development for commuters, you know, really up-market stuff. I was sent to show this guy a house he was after. Bloody lovely place, six beds, all with en suites, jacuzzi, and a thirty foot dining hall. Three acres with stables. That was Steve Morgan. He was a banker from the city, very driven, ambitious, ugly as sin, but dressed lovely and had a Jag. Set my sights, I did, an' got him. I was thirty-one and he was fifty-six, but I didn't care.

Pam hesitated. "I never wanted to be poor ever again, and I needed my mother to see me get married to Steven, see how I lived, so that she would think something of me."

"Where is he now?" asked Tony who was holding her hand.

"Dead… last year."

"So what has made you so sad and ashamed? What does it matter if your family were dirt poor? So what? Loads of people are poor."

"But, my mother hated me, couldn't wait to get rid of me."

"Did you ever think of her and her life? Perhaps

71

she just didn't know how to love. Some people don't or are afraid to. What about you? Have you ever been in love?"

For a moment, Pam couldn't answer because the answer was probably no, and perhaps nobody had loved her either, but she didn't want to tell Tony that. "Perhaps not." She answered slowly and looking like a small child. "I suppose I feel if my mother didn't love me nobody could." Fat tears were rolling down her face. "I just want to be with my animals and to feel safe."

Tony mopped her wet cheeks with a bit of soggy napkin and as he moved closer said, "I have an idea. Something that might just help. Are you up for a bit of adventure?"

"Bloody right I am if it will solve my problems. Anything."

"I thought so. Do you trust me, Pam? "

Fishing a paper tissue from her bag, she blew her nose and dabbed at the mascara runs under her eyes. "I think I do, although you haven't told me much about yourself yet."

"I have pretty much the same background as you except that it was my father who disliked me. Red hair like my mother, you see, and she ran off with a salesman who came to sell us double glazing. I was only three so I don't remember her, but the bitter, old bugger put me into care when I was twelve and by the time I was sixteen, I was into all sorts of petty crime. Learnt a few valuable tricks though. I grew up, got into the car business and did quite well. Worked for a while with a jeweller in Amsterdam, learnt a lot there, I can tell you."

"Jewellery? Diamonds and suchlike?"

Tony nodded. "That's where I met Miguel... my

72

good friend and now my partner in crime, so to speak."

He said this carefully watching Pam's reaction but her eyes were firmly fixed on him and she was listening intently. Tony was pleased, as he was about to reveal his 'dastardly' plan, so he continued. "I got married briefly ten years ago but I was a lousy husband so it didn't last long. Called me a 'fly by night' and I suppose I was. Never been pinned down since. I have had several businesses, the last, a pretty successful one too. Small company supplying luxury accessories for car interiors, you know, things like cocktail coolers, real fur rugs, that sort of thing. Took a partner, Kelvin. He was good at first, but got the gambling bug and to tell the truth, we both overspent. It all collapsed three years ago now. I'm paying off a big loan that he got in the business's name. *He* disappeared with all the assets. In a nutshell that's pretty much it. I have been labouring on a building site for the past year but I have decided to try something a bit more desperate. Shall I tell you?"

"Go on." By this time Pam was intrigued and would not be put off by a bit of skulduggery.

"You might not like it though. It's a bit dangerous."

"Tell me."

"Jewellery."

"Ah ha jewellery. I see the connection. What nicking it?" *Wow, now I really am intrigued,* Pam thought as Tony nodded, took her hand again and walked her forward along the ship's railing.

Pointing upwards, Tony asked, "Can you see the cabin balconies just below the bridge of the ship, fore of the Lido deck? See the second one along? That's number L307 and that is where the Frenchams are. L305 next

73

door is empty, the guy from there left by helicopter couple of days ago after the woman went overboard. Big balconies and accessible with a bit of skill."

"What are you suggesting?"

"I was thinking of relieving them of some of their wealth."

"Are you mad?"

"With your help of course." He smiled engagingly.

"Of course."

"I was just wondering whether with your circus skills you could get from the secluded deck at the front of the ship to the cabin balcony? There is little to hold onto and the fore has a downward slope that could be slippery, but it's not far from the small deck to 307, and you could 'tightrope' the first balcony."

Pam peered upward but couldn't really see in the dark, but Tony continued. "If you could get into the cabin to open the door, I could come in and grab the loot."

"How do you know where it will be? Don't those cabins safes? Mine does."

"Safes are no problem," he replied. "It's getting in and out without being seen, that is the problem, and where to hide the stuff. But as usual I have a great idea." He winked and tapped the side of his nose. Pam laughed as he continued. "If we can get the gear out of the cabin, it will be about the size of a small handbag I reckon, and at a guess about eight hundred thousand pounds' worth. Worth the risk, I'd say."

"Wow, really that much? Split though, I would get half? I will be doing the dangerous bit, after all."

Tony grinned at that. "We'll split it of course 50/50, after I pay off my fence."

"Who?"

Holding up his hands, Tony replied, "One thing at a time. I'll tell you in a bit. Half the final amount is better than where we are now; up to our ears in debt. You could sort out all your problems. What do you say?"

"I make no promises but I'll take a look in the morning." Pam felt her excitement rising. She had no fear of heights and loved the whole idea but she would take a look at the deck and access in the daylight. If they could pull it off, she would at least get her beloved pets back, rent somewhere, and get a job with a bit of money in the bank. It would be a doddle and she wouldn't have to marry a bald-headed dwarf with a big bank account after all. If they got caught, she would end up in jail and her pets would be sold. A daunting thought, but Pam was an optimist despite her failed marriages and lack of a home. She was ready to do anything to save her 'family'.

Tony continued. "It will depend what the dress code is on the night we do it, but if we aim for a casual night they will only have everyday stuff on, not the good stuff. I reckon her diamond necklace alone would bring in about forty-five thousand pounds."

"But everybody will be searched."

"Not if we have an alibi… I will be yours and you will be mine. There are nearly two thousand people on the ship. I don't think they'll search everyone. Anyway they'll think it's an insurance scam, I bet. I know exactly where to hide the loot. There's a ladies toilet on the Lido deck, where the bins are emptied at 5pm. It's the only one that's not emptied twice a day. I've been watching the Frenshams' movements and they're pretty predictable. They leave their cabin at six-ten every evening and don't get back until midnight. Their cabin is second on the list for the cabin boy, but as 305 is empty he goes straight in and is usually out of there at exactly six twenty. That will give us a good window. What do you think so far?"

Pam gazed at him not really quite sure what to say. "You're serious, aren't you?"

"Yes we've got loads of time to plan it. If we can time it right, it'll be easy. Move the stuff the next day before five, by then there will have been a search and we can find somewhere else to stash it until we can get it ashore in Ponta Delgada. There's no security going off the ship, only when you get back on, and have to put everything you're carrying through the x-ray machines. I've already organised a pickup. My very good mate and colleague Miguel is meeting me there. He has a yacht that he sails out of Lisbon to the Azores. Portuguese, you know, and really trustworthy? Miguel is one of the most reliable valuers I've ever met. I'll meet him in Amsterdam and we will sell the gear together. It will take a few weeks but he is a good friend and I know he can be trusted. I've actually used him before." Tony was grinning from ear to ear.

"Really."

"I have to tell you, that I'd already sussed out the Frenshams and how they come to be so darned wealthy. I googled them after I'd first spotted them. It was easy enough to find out about them. One of their biggest money-makers is breeding animals for scientific experimentation. Cats and rabbits mainly, but I also know they have a big, disgusting puppy farm somewhere in Dorset. Makes a mint. It would give me a lot of pleasure to take anything I can from them. I would consider it just desserts for being so fucking… sorry but I do feel strongly about animals… so fucking

76

mercenary." As Tony explained, his face puckered in disgust.

Pam was horrified. "Seriously, you're telling me those gems are the result of animal suffering? Right, I'll help. Tell me what you have planned."

Tony looked relieved. "I was going to use my pickpocketing skills; aiming just for the diamonds. I didn't think for a moment that I would be able to access their cabin. But if you could get in via the balcony, we could do the lot, except what they're wearing of course. It's a risk, but nobody ever locks their balcony doors because there's no access."

His eyes gleamed, and in his excitement, he reached forward and kissed Pam hard on the lips. Startled at first, she resisted but his arms wrapped around her, bringing his body close to hers.

Surprisingly nice, and he smells lovely... *somewhere between apples and ginger biscuits,* she thought as her heart took to beating extra hard and an aching warm tenderness swept through her. *It was a long time since anybody had had that effect on her.*

From then on, Pam and Tony spent every day together. In St Lucia, St Kitts, Guadeloupe, St Maarten and Tortola, they talked and laughed whilst exploring the beaches, towns and markets of the islands. In St Barts they explored Gustavia, the capital, and walked to Shell beach where they swam, collected seashells and ate delicious French / Caribbean cuisine.

Pam no longer looked for a man to keep her. Tony was kind and philosophical about the future, and passionate about his love of animals and so sure everything would work out well. As time went by, her confidence doubled and her resolve to look after herself and her pets grew daily. She had never quite realised that she could be appreciated for anything other than her looks but Tony had a way of making her feel worthy and capable.

Together they made their plans, never doubting that they could succeed. Nothing could be left to chance, every detail had to be precise and perfectly timed.

After leaving the Caribbean islands behind, the days were long and lazy, and along the way, they fell in love. Neither would reveal their feelings of course, and each talked only of when they met up in London to split the cash, Tony to start his own business again and Pam to find a place suitable for herself and her animals.

No mention of a future together.

Sharon and her mother had watched Tony escorting Pam when they went onshore but, as promised kept their distance. Several times, Sharon had surreptitiously given Pam a thumbs up, no doubt thinking that 'Paloma' had found her millionaire. They couldn't hold back their curiosity any longer, and when the ship set sail from the last of the Caribbean islands, they caught Pam in the lift on her way up to the spa to have a massage.

"Pammy... Paloma," Sharon squealed, her fat little face quivering with curiosity. "So, is this the 'one'? Has he got plenty? Come on, tell all."

"Shush... Sharon... No, I don't think he has much, but enough... perhaps. Nice though isn't he?" Pam wasn't going to tell them about Tony's get-rich-quick-plans.

"He's gorgeous and you make a lovely couple,"

gushed Sharon, rolling her eyes and grinning at her mum Hattie, who was chewing on an unlit cigarette. "Isn't he, Mum? Bloody lovely *and* he's smitten with you, Pam, I can tell."

"Do you think so? Look Sha', he isn't what I was looking for. I'm not even sure that he is husband material but I like him, really like him. He knows I'm not really Paloma too. I told him the truth, so you don't have to worry about that. If you like I'll introduce you, see what you think... this afternoon by the pool?"

Hattie rolled the cigarette to the other side of her mouth. "I'll soon tell you if he's the 'one'. I got a good eye for the right bloke."

"She 'as too," laughed Sharon.

That afternoon, Pam introduced Tony to Sharon and Hattie. It seemed the right thing to do and they all had a delightful afternoon getting to know one another. Hattie gave her sign of approval by honking and barking her extraordinary laugh and saying, "Good 'un here, my lovely."

Tony was charming and grinned happily most of the afternoon as the topic ranged from running a market stall, which they did, to the price of corn plasters. They all arranged to meet for dinner that evening.

They had five more days at sea and in that time, Tony and Pam managed to purloin a short length of rope, rubber gloves, a waterproof pouch; someone had left the latter by the pool and Tony thought it must be for an underwater camera and might just come in handy. Both had bought black t-shirts, and Pam a pair of black socks with rubber non-slip pads on the bottom. She already owned black leggings and Tony had black trousers. Every day they watched the movements of the Frenshams, their cabin boy and the little Philippine maid who emptied the bins on the Lido deck. They checked the location of the surveillance cameras, possible hiding places, timed the walk from deck to deck, along corridors and across the pool and bar areas. They practiced everything except the access route across the balconies, which Pam had decided was not nearly as difficult as it looked.

The day before they were due to dock in Ponta Delgada in the Azores, they were ready, and decided that was the right night to do the job as they would dock early the next morning, and as night fell on the 'casual dress' evening, they made their preparations.

The sun had sunk below the horizon and the evening had cooled considerably. Pam and Tony walked to the Riviera bar together, Pam wearing a printed silk kaftan over her black gear and Tony wearing a casual blue shirt over his black t-shirt. They ordered their drinks whilst chatting to the barman whom they hadn't seen before.

"All the better," remarked Tony, "as he is unlikely to remember us."

Taking their drinks to a secluded table away from the bar where there were no surveillance cameras, they sat for a few minutes sipping their drinks.

At exactly six-thirty, Pam made her way past the toilets and the lifts to the door marked 'staff' at the end of the corridor which led to a small area of deck, fore of the Lido deck under the bridge. They had discovered that it

80

was never used by passengers and they had never seen any staff there other than maintenance.

Tony sat reading a newspaper and drinking a soda water that looked like a gin and tonic. Next to his drink sat Pam's Pina colada, and her large, woollen pashmina concealing a sturdy plastic bag. He sipped and waited. There was only one elderly couple in the bar, and few people around as it was now dinnertime. A couple of teenagers were sitting by the pool, busy in conversation.

If they timed everything perfectly, Tony would leave his drink and his newspaper to visit the toilets at exactly seven o'clock, and make his way down the corridor to 307 where he hoped Pam would be waiting with the door open. The cabin boy would have worked his way along from the Frenshams to 355 where Tony knew he would spend about fifteen minutes. That was where the two young women from Blackpool were staying, and although the older one looked like a boy, Tony knew they were a couple from the way they behaved together. He thought they must be particularly untidy as it took several minutes longer than any of the previous cabins.

On reaching the fore deck, Pam felt her nerves for the first time. Although it was dark and there was no one else there, she knew it was a long drop down to the sea from the cabin balconies and her heart did a somersault.

Don't think, just do it Pammy. She could hear Anton's voice as he had shouted at her when she had hesitated on the ropes in France.

Slipping off her kaftan, she rolled it into a small bundle and hid it behind a recliner. Pulling on her gloves, she released the length of rope that she had tucked into her leggings. Reaching up above her head to secure a hold on the downward sloping base of the upper deck, she found little to grip onto. A small ridge gave her enough leverage to get up. Being close to the railings, she only had a few feet to climb to reach the first of the safety rings on the side of the ship that were used when it was being repainted. Pam could see the first one and swung the rope with her left hand to catch the curved rail but missed so tried again.

It didn't seem to be quite long enough but with the third swing, the rope hooked over the rail. Pushing it slowly forward so that it hung down, she leaned to grab it.

The side of the ship sloped away beneath her and for a moment she couldn't breathe as dizziness overcame her. *Steady, stay still for a moment and let it pass.* Anton's voice reached her through her fright. What was she thinking of? But she knew that she had done much more dangerous and much bigger swings in the past, in stunts in the shows in Cavaliere.

Looking along the side of the ship, the balconies seemed to be a long way away, even though she and Tony had scrupulously measured the distance, and knew that it was only a matter of feet between them. She only had one chance to swing the distance, but she knew she could do it easily.

It was already six forty-four, so holding both ends of the rope and twisting them around her right wrist, grabbing the rope with her free hand above her right, she climbed the rail ready to push herself forward to reach the next hold. She only needed to grab it with her left hand and she could then pull herself along and swing her feet onto the first balcony railing. It all had to be done in one movement. Letting go would be the biggest challenge and tightroping along to the next balcony balustrade would require all her concentration and nerve. Checking that there was no one else in sight and without a further thought, she pushed to give her the leverage she needed, swung the few feet, releasing the rope with her left hand and grabbing the second safely bar. As she did so, she heaved with all her might until her left foot made contact with the first cabin balcony. Holding fast, she pulled herself toward the railing and dragged the rope with her. Reaching forward until she could wrap her leg over the top, it took all her strength to pull herself along and grip the rail enough to get onto it. The rope had cut her wrist but as soon as she had pulled herself forward, she gathered it up and stuffed it back into her leggings. The rubber soled socks held her firmly on the rail.

The next part was relatively simple and once she stood upright on the balcony rail of 305, she confidently walked the ten feet to the end and held steady while she checked the one grab rail and the shorter distance to swing. It had only taken twelve minutes thus far, so she had plenty of time. The lights were still on in cabin 307; she could see the glow on the balcony railing.

Pam took a deep breath and slowed her fast-beating heart, knowing that adrenaline was flooding her body ready for the next action. She hesitated, knowing that in six minutes, Tony would be outside the door waiting for her. In a moment of panic she thought, *What if the Frenshams are still there or the cabin boy is ? I'll give him a heart attack.*

Suddenly the light went out and Pam breathed with relief. Without a pause, she swung across to the balcony of 307 and linked her leg easily before pulling herself over. It was now exactly three minutes past seven. Tony had calculated that from the bar to 307 would take precisely three minutes. Slowly standing and moving toward the doors, Pam turned the handle easily and stepped into the now-dark cabin. She started to shake, as the realisation at what she had done swept over her. She felt like crying or screaming; the aftermath of the adrenalin rush she knew, but she held her hand over her mouth and crept toward the door to the spy hole to check if Tony was there, and that there was no one else around. The plan was that he would walk on and out to the deck if there was anyone in the corridor and wait until it was clear.

He wasn't there. She waited. Panic gripped her and she felt that something awful had happened. Turning, she surveyed the room. It was a mess and it didn't look as if the cabin boy had been in. The bed was a pile of crumpled sheets and discarded clothing. Perhaps they slept in the afternoon but why hadn't the boy made the bed?

Quite suddenly, Pam heard the sound of a key being inserted into the door and she turned and leapt out onto the balcony, pulling the doors behind her as quietly as she could. The lights went on and she could hear a faint whishing of bedding and things being moved around.

The clatter of hangers in the wardrobe made her jump followed by the bathroom taps and toilet being flushed. Looking at her watch in the dim light, she could see that it was already ten past seven. She stayed frozen, pushing her body into the wall of the balcony as the curtains were pulled shut.

What if the door was locked? She would have to return the way she had come and at that moment didn't think she could find the strength. Fifteen minutes past seven. Her legs were shaking as she waited for the light to go out and the door to close. *What am I doing stuck on a strange balcony when I should be dressed having a luxurious pre-dinner cocktail in the Horizon bar? What the hell's gone wrong? Everything's been planned down to the last detail.*

Pam was cold now, the temperature having dropped considerably in the last few days. She stood for a moment undecided, their plans became a blizzard of whirling panic. *Have I got the timing wrong?* she wondered as the jittery sensation in her limbs increased. She felt queasy at the thought of being caught. She had a faint sense of unreality but hearing the sound of the ocean and distant music from the bar, brought her to her senses and she thought about the money that would make such a difference to her life.

The light went out. Silence. *Come on, take a chance. Think of your pets. If nothing else get out of this cabin, even if you have to make a run for it.*

She tried the door but her hands were shaking and wet with perspiration. Rubbing them on her hips, she tried again and this time the balcony door opened and she moved toward the tiny spy hole in the door. *Please be there, Tony.*

The service trolley was just moving and she could hear it being wheeled away. Seven   twenty...   one... two... three. Then, there he was. Pam could hardly breathe with relief as she opened the door and he slipped into the cabin, his face flushed with anxiety. Grabbing

85

her hand, he whispered, "Don't ask. Your job is done you clever girl, now get out, get your kaftan and get back to the bar. I'll be back in a few minutes."

Pam found herself in the empty corridor, the two surveillance cameras covered, one with a black sock and the other with Tony's blue shirt, and quickly made her way back to the fore deck, slipping on her kaftan.

Within minutes, and without seeing a soul, she was back in the bar sipping the now-warm Pina colada. The rope that was tucked into her leggings was carefully removed and popped into the plastic bag with the rubber gloves.

There were still only a few couples in and around the deck. The teenagers by the pool had disappeared, but a group had gathered at the far end of the bar and were drinking and playing cards so it was unlikely that they would notice anything about Pam and Tony's movements.

Tony re-appeared holding the pouch, which he quickly put into the plastic bag and covered with Pam's pashmina. It had taken him exactly eight minutes to reappear back into his seat in the bar. He smiled, picked up his drink and said happily, "Cheers, lovely Paloma. Do you want another drink?"

Pam couldn't speak and looked at Tony in amazement. He was calm and pleased with himself. Her legs were still shaking and her heart had only slowed a beat or two, but here he was looking as though he hadn't a care in the world. She noticed he was wearing only one black sock, the other hung out of his trouser pocket.

She grinned. "What took you so long?" she said finally and started to laugh, a feeling of such relief bubbling up from her insides. It was amazing that it was over. She covered her face with her hands. "I nearly died of fright when the cabin boy was late."

Tony took her shaking hands and lowered them so he could look into her eyes. "He wasn't late, I am *so* sorry, but it was his night off. I should have checked. It was the one thing I hadn't thought of. I really thought the cabin boys only got time off when we were in dock. The maid did the cabins tonight and she was late. Stupid of me, but no worries, here we are." He indicated the purple pashmina carefully folded over the bag. "Next step. You need to take a trip to the ladies."

Without hesitating, Pam picked up the bag, tucked it under one arm and wrapped the pashmina around her shoulders and upper arms, then walked as confidently as she could to the ladies toilet. There were several ladies in the room, three of them gossiping about a couple who had very nearly been robbed and beaten up in Guadeloupe. Another was rolling lipstick around her pouted lips and at least two cubicles were occupied. Pam walked into the end cubicle and sat down and waited. It took nearly ten minutes for the ladies room to empty, and quickly she pushed the bag down to the bottom of the waste-bin and covered it with discarded paper towels. She breathed a sigh of relief. One more step completed.

When Pam made her way back to the bar, Tony had risen and was talking to Hattie who was puffing on her after-dinner ciggie.

"No we haven't eaten yet... just going... Here she is now." Turning to Pam with a wink, he continued. "Hattie's asking if we are going on any of the trips in Ponta Delgada tomorrow."

"I don't think we are actually, Hattie. We are going

to take a wander on our own. What about you?" she asked, hoping that they were already booked on something. The last thing that they wanted was Sharon and Hattie tagging along with them. They were meeting Miguel at 10.30am on his yacht in the marina and Tony said they would be expected to stay for lunch and possibly have a trip around the bay.

It suddenly occurred to Pam that she had no idea exactly what she had just deposited in the waste-bin. *Was there enough? Could we get it back? Can we get it off the ship to deliver it to Miguel. Will it be enough to get my pets back and pay off Tony's debts?*

There was still a long way to go before she could relax.

By then, people were coming out from the first sitting of dinner, and were filling the bar when Sharon appeared with drinks for the four of them, but Pam suddenly felt hungry. "Sharon, thanks, so kind of you, but we need to eat. Shall we see you later?"

"OK, Pammie, laters then. We'll be 'ere. The band will arrive in a bit. We're dancing tonight… come straight back, both of you. I have just learned 'ow to rumba in the dance class today, so want to 'ave a go at it." Sharon giggled, rotating her hips so that she slopped the drinks.

"Go girl, go," laughed Hattie.

Tony and Pam laughed too, waved as they left with promises of dancing later. They almost ran down the stairs to the lifts on B deck. "Let's go eat and you can explain what happened. You were so quick." Pam said breathlessly as they jumped in the empty lift going down to the dining room.

Tony was smiling. "It was all packed in the one bag and the safe wasn't even locked. I couldn't believe it. I didn't even have a chance to really look in it, but I think it's all there, the rubies, diamonds, watches and some stuff I haven't seen before. Oh, PammyPaloma, my lovely girl, we did it." At that point, he let his excitement loose and wrapped his arms around her, while his feet did a little dance. He lifted her off her feet, just at the point where the lift stopped, the doors opened and to the amusement of the waiting passengers, Tony and Pam waltzed out together.

The waiter found them a table on their own and they ordered a bottle of the best of Jamie Quendera from a Portuguese winemaker that Tony said was a friend of Miguels. It was called 'Dona Ermelinda' and the crisp, citrusy flavour suited their mood perfectly. They were so happy. In between courses, Pam explained how she had got to the cabin whilst Tony kept telling her how brave and clever she was.

"You were amazing, Pammy. What a bloody great team we make."

"It's not over yet. How can you be so relaxed about it? It could still be found. and we have to get it off the ship."

"Even if it was found, there is nothing to link us to it, is there? After breakfast tomorrow we will retrieve it and if we need to find another hiding place. I've found just the spot. No worries."

The waiter arrived with the coffee and as he left, Pam whispered, "Where are you going to hide it? Tell me."

"Nope, but we will disembark with it safely tucked

in your beach bag so let's just enjoy the evening and worry about it all tomorrow."

Pam's expression changed to one of slight suspicion, her heart beating painfully in her chest. Just for a moment she thought that he could be planning to run off with it all himself, so she asked gently, "We are going to do it together, aren't we, Tony?"

Taking her hands and looking into her worried face, he smiled and answered, "Of course we are. You're not thinking that I would run out on you are you? I couldn't even if I wanted to. The time we have spent together has been the happiest of my life, don't you know that? Now, drink your coffee as I want to kiss you."

Pam felt her insecurities slipping away. He really was the most charming, exciting and lovely man she had ever met. Perhaps now was the time to put their relationship on an altogether different footing. Up until that night, she had kissed him at the end of the evening and gone to her bed alone, sure that the relationship should be kept on a business level. Tony had not once suggested that they might have a future together but it was becoming clear that they had very strong feelings for each other.

The excitement of their daring and adventurous escapade added to the magic of their first night spent together.

For the first time ever, Pam felt cherished and adored, and as they made love, Tony's desire for her extinguished thoughts of anything other than the joy of the moment. As they explored each other, tentatively at first, then with extraordinary passion, she realised that she had never felt this way in her life, certainly not with Joe or Steven or even sexy Paulo. Pam was no longer acting at being loving and sexy, what she was experiencing felt real and natural.

Even so, as the night wore on and they were wrapped, happy and exhausted, in each other's arms, Pam's insecurities were there, lurking in the back of her mind. *Could this be real? Am I really falling in love so fast. Does he really care for me or is it only that I have helped him get money to pay his debt?* so she asked carefully, "Do you think having a relationship at this point is wise. You might feel differently when we get back."

Tony smiled and turned to face her. "Actually," he said, "I think it is the best possible answer for both of us. We need someone special in our lives, don't we? We need tying down to a real relationship. One that hasn't anything to do with debts or business or even pets. Perhaps that has been missing for both of us. I told you we are a brilliant team." He laughed out loud. "You, my lovely Paloma, are the feistiest, most beautiful, brave and clever woman I have ever met. And… I adore you. There I've said it."

"Oh," was all Pam could say but it confirmed that they would not say goodbye when the ship docked in Southampton or when they met up to divide the proceeds, and she was deliriously happy at the prospect.

The excitement of being together, and the plans for the following day kept them awake and consequently they had very little rest. Rising early, they made their preparations to collect the jewels and disembark.

Pam was nervous and felt slightly sick at the prospect of being caught or questioned. She didn't have any idea how she would react if she was interrogated.

Stop worrying, she told herself. She knew she could act if she wanted to. *My whole life until now had been an act, hasn't it? But last night changed everything. I'm not sure I can trust myself anymore. I want to be real from now on.*

She had only managed to swallow a cup of coffee that morning, whereas Tony had eaten well; demolishing bacon, eggs and toast and didn't seem worried at all. Her limbs ached from the exertion of the night before, and her wrist was sore and red from the rope burn, so she wore a large silver bangle over it.

"Sharon and Hattie will want to know why we didn't go back for the dancing last night. Shall we tell them?" Pam asked as they collected their things to go onshore.

"Course we'll tell them, the after dinner bit, not the rest." Tony laughed and pulled her close. "I want the world to know how I feel about you. But let's get today over first and then we can relax and enjoy the rest of the cruise. We will be able to make some seriously good plans. We'll get your dogs and horses back, and I will pay off my debts."

"Oh, Tony I can't believe that we could be rich."

"We're going to be loaded. How do you feel about opening a haven for abused animals? It's something I have always dreamed of."

" Really? What a great idea. I've secretly always wanted to do something with animals. But I am so scared of getting caught now I can't think any further than today."

"Tomorrow then we will make plans. Let's go."

The weather forecast predicted early rain but then

brilliant sunshine in the afternoon, so Pam was carrying the beach bag with a raincoat for each of them and Tony had an umbrella tucked under his arm. As yet there was no rain but storm clouds were gathering on the horizon.

Taking Pam's hand, he led her to the lift that would take them to the Lido deck.

To their surprise, there was no sign of an alarm being raised, searches being made or of questions being asked, so they walked around the bar and pool area to see if there was any action there.

The temperature was considerably cooler and there was only one stalwart swimmer doing his lengths in the pool, cleaners and waiters were attending to the tables and stowing away the sunshades and chairs but there were few others around and no sign of any alarm.

Tony looked perplexed, expecting at least some delay before passengers were allowed off-board but no, nothing at all. "OK, Pam, go get the gear. We've an interesting day ahead of us."

Pam gulped, but marched off determinedly towards the ladies room, and within minutes had the bag pushed under the raincoats. It was now only a matter of getting them off the ship.

The great cruiser docked in Ponta Delgada at about nine am, and passengers were lined up waiting to disembark. Everything looked peaceful except for the stormy grey clouds rushing toward them.

Pam and Tony joined the queue, went down the steps and strolled happily along the dock toward the main road. They could hardly contain their excitement as they had not been stopped or searched, and the only comment made was by a passing crew member who said casually, "Have a good day, folks," as they passed him at the bottom of the steps.

The Frenshams were fast asleep in their untidy cabin. Clothes and shoes strewn around the floor, jewellery scattered across the dressing table. 'Frenchie' and 'Goldie" Frensham had had a skin-full the previous night as they had had some bad news from home the day before. Their puppy farm had been closed by the local authorities, which meant a considerable decline in their already diminishing income. Only the week before the cruise, an official letter from the cancer research company that they supplied with rabbits and cats, wrote that, due to public pressure, they were limiting their order for live animals as from that month. Frenchie and Goldie had drowned their sorrows with several bottles of wine and one of brandy, and hadn't retuned to their cabin until the dancing was finished at one am. 'Goldie' liked to dance and 'Frenchie' liked to watch her especially when she had had a 'few'.

At nine-thirty, they were just stirring by which time the wind had risen and the skies opened.

Fat drops of rain were falling, bursting into little fountains on the pavement, and people were running for shelter. Many of the passengers were jumping onto buses for the island tours, but Tony and Pam, who was holding the bag of jewellery firmly against her chest, ran like teenagers, along the main road toward the marina where they were to meet Miguel. Even the raincoats and the umbrella failed to keep them dry. They looked like they might have come straight out of the sea. They slowed down at the first coffee shop and decided to wait a little till the storm abated. They sat dripping, laughing and relieved. It was only half past nine.

Goldie looked out of the cabin window. "Don't think we'll bother to go on shore, Frenchie. Just look at the pissing rain," and she turned back into the pile of crumpled bedding and fell back into a deep slumber.

The heavy rain abated, but still it drizzled, and Tony and Pam couldn't wait to open their parcel any longer, so they raced to the marina and found the yacht easily amongst the hundreds there. It was called 'Abundance'.

How very apt, thought Pam. Miguel was waiting, tall, tanned and handsome and at least sixty.

He was surprised to see Pam with Tony so early but welcomed them both with hugs and kisses,, and drew them into the inside seating area, taking their wet clothes and supplying towels to dry themselves.

"So good to see you, Tony, and who is your lovely companion?"

Scrubbing his head with the towel, Tony replied, "This lady is Paloma, and she is the bravest, most wonderful person I have ever met. She helped me in the most amazing way, so she is now my partner in crime. Because of her, we have a huge haul. Wait till you see," and turning to Pam added, "This is it, my lovely. We are about to see 'the fruits of our labour'."

The excitement was intense, and together they explained to Miguel what they had done and how. Within minutes, they had the bag opened on the table, pouring out its contents. Pam had never seen such an array of jewels: a ruby and diamond necklace, sapphire and diamond brooches and earrings, a brooch of huge emeralds and diamonds, another set with pink diamonds. Little boxes contained rings with every sort of gem imaginable, but the most beautiful of all was the diamond necklace and earrings with at least two to three carats in every diamond.

Miguel had his magnifying glass ready and stuck it into place on his right eye. Picking up the diamond necklace first, he gasped.

Tony smiled at Pam, assuming that Miguel was impressed with the quality of their haul. They were holding hands, sweaty with excitement.

Miguel moved the gems around and grimly handed the magnifying glass and necklace to Tony. "Fake, very good of course, definitely fake. Really good copy though, and in itself worth several hundred pounds, but sadly not thousands."

"What?" spluttered Tony as he snatched up the gems to study.

"Sorry, this too," said Miguel eyeing the huge 'emerald and diamond' ring. Picking up another necklace, he shook his head again. "Copies."

"Jeez, Miguel… You're kidding me. Is there nothing of any value?"

Miguel was slowly working through the pile and found two rings that were worth a few thousand each and the gold chains and bracelets would bring in a few hundred. One old necklace had several worthy diamonds, and Miguel estimated that they could get about six thousand. The whole lot would bring them about forty thousand pounds. Not much, and by the time Miguel had taken his cut... less than twenty thousand each for Pam and Tony. Not a lot less than if he had not had Pam's support, and had only managed to purloin the diamond necklace that was his original plan. Except that it wasn't real... so they had done well to make a profit at all.

Stunned as they were, Tony started to laugh. He couldn't control himself and despite her disappointment, Pam started to giggle too, although hers was more of a release of pent-up nervous energy. Tony was genuinely amused. Soon the three of them were howling at the whole adventure and all Tony could say was, "Thank God we didn't get caught. Still can't believe the Frenshams haven't discovered it's missing, even though it's fake... I bet they won't even report it. They will claim on the insurance. Can you imagine trying to explain... I'd like to bet on it though. Oh, Pam, my darling, what are we going to do?

Did this mean we have no future together? was Pam's only thought. She gulped and the tears started – she couldn't stop them. Tony stopped laughing and Miguel appeared with tissues and a large brandy each.

"Pammy, my lovely don't cry. Here drink this... We'll still be together and I promise you we'll find a way to get the dogs and the horses back. I'll work my socks off so that you can, I promise you. I'll do anything to make it possible." Tony held her tight while she sobbed into his chest.

Pam sniffed and blew her nose, gulped the brandy and lifting her chin, Tony gazed into her lovely brown eyes, her makeup had disappeared in the rain and her wet hair was hanging in dripping curtains, flat against her head. Look at you, all real, you look beautiful. I am so happy to know you, PammyPaloma."

Pam lifted her hand to his cheek. "You look pretty beautiful yourself," she said and she felt as if the sun was bursting through the clouds. "My tall, red-headed hero, failed-jewellery-thief. I thought you were going to drape me in diamonds." Before she could stop herself she added laughingly. "I'll get a job too and work to help you." She couldn't believe what she was saying, but she did genuinely mean it. For the first time ever in her adult life, she wanted happiness not just for herself but also for this lovely man she had discovered would starve himself to make her happy.

Tony ran his fingers across her lips and Pam shivered with pleasure, slipped her hands around his neck and pulled him down to her. She clung to him as he kissed her tenderly.

"Let's get married, put what we've managed to get to good use, rent somewhere with a field, I don't care where we go as long as its together. I can build you a stable. I will get a job, day and night if necessary."

"What did you say, Tony? Get married?" Pam sniffed, hardly able to believe her ears. "Are you suggesting we get married without enough for us to live on, never mind support the pets... to get married, with your debts? Seriously?" But she was grinning as he replied.

"Yes, I am. I'll find a way to pay off my debts. I love and adore you, and I want to make you happy. Will we do it?"

Pam's heart gave a surge of aching warm tenderness towards Tony. She felt as if the sun was shining on them despite the clouds of disappointment, so it took Pam less than a minute to make up her mind to say yes. She no longer felt the need to have a life full of pretence just so that she could selfishly have what she wanted. "OK, yes I will, but I'll sell the horses if I have to. Must keep George and Didi though. Can we do that?"

"We'll keep them all. We'll find a way you'll see."

"Legally or Illegally?" she laughed.

"Whatever... but although we've failed to make a fortune, I've found you. I promise you now I'll make it up to you." Pam's heart was full to overflowing. It all seemed so silly and romantic and she wasn't quite sure whether it wasn't all too crazy, just like their 'gone-wrong heist' but no amount of disappointment could take away the good feeling that was sweeping through them at that moment.

"I will want to see you sometimes and I won't if you work morning noon and night. Yes, let's get married as soon as we can."

"Good, that's settled then," said Miguel. "We'll celebrate now, if not for being rich, but for being happy and in love. You are two lucky people *and* you can choose yourself a ring, eh Pam? "said Miguel indicating the pile of 'loot' twinkling on the table.

"Are you married, Miguel?" asked Pam with a teasing smile. "You look as if you have a bob or two." Tony and Miguel laughed.

"Hey, come here you crazy woman," Tony said happily, as he wrapped his arms around his new-found treasure. Pick a ring and we keep it 'til we get home so that it won't be recognised, but we will tell Sharon and Hattie, they will be ecstatic for us, and we could have a bit of a party before we get back to Southampton. They like a bit of romance on these cruises.

His mind was made up. No more silly schemes, no

more get-rich-quick ideas. Perhaps they could work with animals somewhere that. could take the horses and the dogs. Life was wonderful…

***

What Pam didn't know as she made her decision on that wet day in Ponta Delgarda, was that one of the grubby lottery tickets lurking in the bottom of her handbag was worth just slightly over a million pounds, and what Tony didn't know when he promised to starve himself to pay off his debts, and help Pam keep her animals was that his beloved, rich godfather had died the previous week and left him a five acre farm in Yorkshire.

***

OLIVIA & CAROLINE – Out There

"Are they are a couple, do you think, Olly?" Caroline asked indicating the rather good-looking pair laughing together as they walked towards the Riviera bar. She had watched them for over an hour as they sat by the pool, talking, flirting and then in deep, serious conversation.

The lady in the pretty sundress, and hair like a ripe conker was upset, and Caroline had watched the tall red-haired man lean forward and gently wipe her tears.

"No, I saw them boarding. They weren't together then. I think they must have met on the ship but they have done pretty much all the islands together. Saw them in Tortola on the beach."

"They've been talking non-stop. Do you think he's upset her?"

"Don't know."

"No I don't think he has. I've watched him and he's been listening, really listening to her talking... opening her heart about something, I would guess. Most men don't really listen, do they?"

"Nah, fucking never listen, do they?"

"But he really has. As if he cared about what she was saying. Have you noticed, most couples hardly talk to each other. It's as if after years, they have run out of things to say. These two are just finding out about each other. They make a nice couple. And he is rather gorgeous."

"What! Oh God, I hope you're not back into blokes are you?"

"Oh, no never again. I've been playing at being a hetero for too long. Don't you worry about that."

Caroline smiled reassuringly at Olivia who took hold of her hand, "Good. I don't want you to ever change your mind."

She only occasionally had doubts about Caroline's commitment to her new status.

"I'm just so happy to be here with you, Olly. I've never been so happy. It's taken me a long time to know who I am and what I want. I married for all the wrong reasons and I know Elliot will be devastated but I think he knew before I did. I never want to go back to that pretence again." Then she added, "Do you think we will run out of things to say to each other, Olly you and I?"

"Probably at the end of the century," Olivia laughed as she crossed her neatly trousered legs. "Oh, I guess it happens that at some point we know everything about each other... no need to talk. I think that some of the people on this ship have been together over fifty years by the looks of them."

As if the 'fates' had to provide the answer, the cruise director and entertainment manager, Glen Travis, was setting up games and encouraging people sitting around to take part, shouted, "Right, we are looking for couples who have been married for the longest. Anyone here been married over sixty years? Yes, yes, I see a couple over there. Heidi..." He indicated his colleague holding the microphone in the direction of the small shrivelled hand waving from the lower deck.

"So how long have you been married, sir, madam? Sixty one... well I never. Can anyone beat that? No? Then you automatically get a prize, my dears. A round of applause please." A bottle of champagne appeared and was presented by Heidi to the elderly husband whose wife had sunk back down into her wheelchair.

"Any anniversaries or birthdays? OK here we have… " Glen pushed the microphone toward a couple. "Sally and Ben. Anniversary… twelve years today. Twelve years, did you say? Past the seven year itch then? Ha, ha. Congratulations. Let's say it with a song," and on cue there was Cliffy singing 'Congratulations' to which everyone joined in as Sally and Ben, waving and grinning, collected a bottle of champagne.

Several boisterous games followed, and most people took the fun into their stride. Silly clothes were donned for races in and around the pool, bawdy songs were sung and the more extrovert of the passengers danced to Abba, Queen, Tina Turner, and a lively version of YMCA.

Olivia and Caro danced along with the best of them. They were after all amongst the youngest there.

"Last one!" shouted Glen. "Any couple here madly in love? Yes, one or two I see. OK then, first pair in the pool gets the prize. Go, go, go…."

Olly raised an enquiring eyebrow to Caro and grinning, she nodded her assent. They grabbed each other's hand and ran laughing toward the pool.

'Yahooing' loudly, they jumped and caused a tidal wave. No one else but an elderly couple joined them, and they slithered slowly down the steps trying to avoid the great splash that the two girls had made.

"A big round of applause please… and the prize goes to… " Glen approached the pool and maintaining a thoroughly professional attitude, leant forward and pushed the microphone toward them as they surfaced together.

Spluttering, Caroline shouted as loudly as she could, "Caro and Olly.

The happiest couple on the ship."

***

FRANK – Enduring Love

'What a terrible end to a lovely day.' Frank's body has gone into a state of shock and Geraldine and Brian were trying to force a large brandy into him. He could hear Geraldine's soothing tone urging him to drink. It was as if he was in a deep fog, but he opened his mouth and felt the liquid burn his throat and sending a hot glow downward towards his frozen heart. Poor sweet Edith, what had happened to her?

"Was it sunstroke, do you think?" he heard himself ask.

"No, no, she has had some sort of stroke, but they don't think it has anything to do with the sun," Geraldine replied.

Edith was always careful, and that day on the beach in St Lucia she had been covered with sunscreen, worn her hat, and except for her quick dip in the sea had stayed out of the sun all day.

"They won't let me go with her. Why not?" Frank asked." She will wake up and be surrounded by strangers. She will be frightened."

"They'll get in touch with her husband," answered Brian.

"Dear God, so they will. I never thought of that." Frank realised then that their secret would probably emerge, as Edith's husband William would surely fly out to take her back home for treatment.

For six years now, he and Edith had been meeting once a year for a month-long cruise together, and for Frank, it was the one thing he looked forward to in life. He saved every penny so that he could meet up with

Edith, whom he loved dearly. His own wife Margaret had died three years before and had never known of the arrangement. She had accompanied Frank on their first cruise four years earlier when they had first met the other couples; Edith and William, and Geraldine and Brian, but she had hated every minute of it, as had William. William was a diabetic, had had a knee and a hip replacement and was very seasick so swore he would never do another cruise. In February every year, Edith left William for a month in the Caribbean with Frank. For the rest of the year, she took good care of her ailing husband. She would never leave William of course, and however much Frank wanted it, he had ceased to ask.

"William has been a good husband to me and we've been married since we were teenagers. We knew a long time ago that we shouldn't have married but we're now good friends and I will never desert him. We were so young and so very different, but by that time we had four children and I put aside my needs to be a good mother and wife," Edith had told Frank on their first cruise together as a couple, and it was now agreed that if ever anything happened to William, Edith would move to Edinburgh to be with Frank. Her grown-up children were spread: two in the Northeast, one in Canada and one in the Lake District where Edith lived with William.

Frank had one son, Jeremy, whom he rarely saw and he too lived in Windermere with his husband Simon, a person Frank had failed to like even though he had tried on many occasions. He was not opposed to his son's choices or way of life, but found Simon judgemental and intolerant and now that Margaret had gone, contact had diminished. Jeremy knew that his father Frank didn't get on with Simon but he also knew that Frank loved him and would always be there for him. Frank had made that very clear four years before when Jeremy had married Simon.

As far as Frank was concerned, Edith had become the focus of his life and their once-a-year cruise together was the happiest time of both their lives, but for Frank, although he hated to admit it, he lived for the days he spent with Edith. They adored each other's company, liked doing the same things, and found the cruise and the Caribbean a delight. Over the years they had explored many of the islands and Edith was writing a pensioners guide to 'Enjoying and Being Safe in the Caribbean.'

That morning they had explored the Derek Walcott Square near the centre of Castries, visited the Cathedral of the 'Immaculate Conception' and the Carnegie Library, collecting information for Edith's book, and ended up on a charming beach at Vigie, to the north of the town.

They met Geraldine and Brian, at the harbour entrance as they returned from their day out.

"Had a good day, you two?" Brian asked with a twinkle. It had been a constant source of amusement since meeting up on the first cruise that Edith and Frank did together, without the partners that they had met on the cruise the year before.

They had both been very candid about their feelings for each other, and explained simply that neither William nor Margaret ever wanted to cruise again, and that their holiday together was as far as the relationship would go for the time being. It was now Brian and Geraldine's secret too and meeting up every year since had become the norm.

"Great day… just lovely," replied Frank, smiling broadly at Edith who had slowed down a little. He took her arm and addressed Brian and Geraldine. "Want to meet for a drink before dinner? Tell you all about it?"

At the steps of the cruise ship, Edith stopped, put her hand to her head, dropped her bag and collapsed. As Frank had hold of her arm, he too crumpled and ended up on the ground. Brian was quick to help him up, but Edith did not recover. Frank lifted Edith's head and whispered. "Oh my love, my love…" over and over. The right side of her face sagged and a sliver of dribble trickled onto Frank's hand. Her eyes were fluttering and she was moaning softly.

Brian raced up the gangplank, and luckily the ship's doctor was at hand who quickly recognised the symptoms of a stroke, and organised an ambulance to take her to the Victoria Hospital in Castries.

Frank was firmly informed by the paramedics that only next of kin were allowed to accompany patients to the hospital, and even though he had tried to explain that they were travelling together, he was refused access to the ambulance. Frank was distraught. Brian told him that he would have to get back on the ship as it was sailing in less than two hour's time to St Kitts, the next port of call. Edith would have to wait for William to come and take her home.

Panic gripped Frank. *What of her clothes and possessions that were in their cabin and her passport in his pocket? What if she didn't recover? He wouldn't even be able to say goodbye. Perhaps they would never meet again.* A great sense of loss overcame Frank and he couldn't, wouldn't, accept that. He decided straight away that he must stay and make sure nothing dreadful happened to her and even if it meant facing William, his beloved Edith must be looked after.

"No, Brian I'm staying." he informed his friends.

"What about the rest of the cruise? You'll miss–"

"I'll miss Edith. Nothing would be the same without her. I have decided to stay."

Brian shrugged. "Perhaps you are right, old boy. Edith needs you now. Better hurry though as the ship will be sailing soon. You need to see the Bursar and explain. Come on then, I'll give you a hand."

Together Geraldine, Brian and Frank made the necessary arrangements for Frank to leave the ship, and the Bursar even suggested somewhere for Frank to stay near the hospital. They packed everything carefully making sure Edith's clothes and possessions were in the right place. She was very particular and tidy so Frank made sure not to disappoint her with his packing.

An hour later, the ship sailed on towards St Kitts, and Frank stood on the dockside surrounded by cases, watching it leave. A single tear trickled down his suntanned cheek.

Together he and Edith had had such a wonderful, loving time together he could not abandon her now. He easily found a taxi. The Hilltop View guesthouse that the Bursar had recommended was clean and bright and the manageress was sympathetic and kind when he explained that he didn't know how long he would be staying, and briefly told her the situation.

However much he tried he could *not* get access into the hospital ward where Edith lay. Eventually a fat, little, brown nurse called Pempera, seeing how distressed

Frank was, took pity on him, and went to find a progress report and an update on the situation.

To his relief, Edith was conscious and Pempera had made her aware that he was there and would get to her whenever possible.

"Is she going to recover?" he asked when Pempera returned with the news.

"Partially I'm sure, but man, it was a severe stroke and usually patients need a lot o' care, especially in de beginnin'. With physio and support it will mos' likely be possible for her to walk and speak again some time in de future."

"Thank you, Pempera, you have been most kind."

"I 'ave to tell you, man " she said quietly. "Her 'usband is arriving tomorrow at midday."

To Pempera's surprise Frank answered. "Good, I am pleased to hear that." She had very quickly recognised the situation and felt sorry for this kindly, elderly gentleman, whose love for Edith shone out of him whenever he spoke her name.

"Will you stay, man?"

"Yes, until she leaves."

William was not a well man and the flight had been difficult for him. He was overweight, hot and uncomfortable but even so very concerned about Edith.

Arriving at the hospital, intent on finding which ward Edith was on, William passed by Frank without noticing him. Frank knew instantly that this was Edith's husband, six years older, heavier, with a florid complexion, wheezing and sweating as he hurried past.

Frank was concerned. How would he care for Edith? Perhaps she would have go permanently into care.

110

The thought made Frank gasp with worry. He knew what a living death that would be for Edith who was so intelligent, happy and full of life. Or at least she had been.

On seeing his wife so stricken, unable to talk or move her right side, all William could feel was panic. She had always been so fit and healthy, and it was she, who looked after him. Before leaving England, he had made arrangements for her to go into their local hospital when they returned, but what about after that? He tried to reassure her that he would cope and get her the very best help possible, but his heart was full of despair.

In the coffee shop downstairs, Frank was thinking hard. He sat with a sliced peach on a plate in front of him and a cup of weak tea that he had ordered an hour before,. He was watching the lift doors, undecided what to do. *Should I sneak away now that William is here to take care of her or wait? Should I satisfy myself about Edith's on-going care by announcing myself to William? Perhaps that would distress William even more if he knew about me, and reject Edith altogether. I just don't know how William will react to the knowledge that I have been part of her life all these years. No, I 'll wait for a while, perhaps another day or two.*

Frank's thoughts raced around his head. It was now early evening and little Pempera was going off duty, but seeing him, she paused and told him. "No change man. Her 'usband is with 'er now. Go get some rest, eh."

Perhaps she was right. Frank had hardly slept the night before and had arrived at the hospital at seven am. Most of the day he had spent in the coffee shop. Perhaps after good meal and some sleep, everything would be

111

clearer in the morning. Pempera had told him that it was unlikely that Edith would be moved for a few days at least.

On returning to The Hilltop View and showering away the smell of the hospital, Frank walked down to the bay area, marvelling again at the beauty of the island with its shimmering golden sands, its towering bird of paradise flowers and ferns, banks of bougainvillea and whitewashed buildings. It was very similar to where he and Edith had enjoyed the afternoon of their trip out the day before.

He found a noisy back street cafe that sold local lobster dishes with bread-fruit chips, and fresh figs for dessert. A glass of cold, local beer and Frank was ready for bed.

It was still very hot, but the walk back was short and within minutes he was outside the Hilltop View again. Entering the small foyer he was wondering whether Edith was comfortable or whether he should go back to the hospital, when a voice interrupted. "Hello Frank. I knew you wouldn't be far away."

Frank caught his breath, not quite knowing how to respond. It was the last thing he had expected. He was face-to-face with William, who was holding out a hand. He had changed from his travelling clothes and was wearing a pair of baggy shorts and a comfortable shirt. He looked better now than he had at lunchtime.

"Ah, William." Frank took his hand. *So he had known about us all along.* "You knew? William I… I'm sorry… really I am." Frank stuttered finding it hard to believe, but Edith had never given any indication of knowing that William was aware of their arrangement.

"No need, you obviously care for her, after all this is the sixth year. I am sure you know... "

"That long?"

"Yes, ever since the first year, I have known. Edith didn't tell me, didn't need to. You took some lovely photos on your first cruise together and she was a bit careless about putting them away. I was angry at first, but you both looked so happy and relaxed with each other. I really expected her to leave, you know." William added. "Oh, she knows you are here by the way. I told her and the little nurse confirmed it. She told me where you were staying too. Wise little woman, that Pempera. Asked a lot of questions first." He gave a short laugh at the recollection of Pempera's words. 'No trouble now'.

"Come on, let's have a drink." William indicated the bar around the corner.

Together they walked in and ordered a couple of beers.

"I must say this is a surprise. I was really worried... I didn't know how you would feel if I stayed," Frank said as they took the drinks to a table outside.

"Relieved I can tell you... yes, relieved, that she was with somebody she knew and who cared about her. I wasn't sure that you would stay. I am grateful that you did, although I understand that they won't let you see her." William was gazing into his glass with a sad expression.

"No, next of kin only."

There was a long silence whilst they drank their beers. The night noises increased as people made their way out of the bars and restaurants to go home.

William looked at his watch. "It's getting late. I'll go back in the morning."

But he wanted to talk to Frank so that he understood. He didn't want Frank to feel guilty.

"Edith and I are good friends you know, but... anyway, yes, fond of each other but not for a long time... well, you know. It didn't change things for us, her going away with you. In fact her having a break made it better. It... you, made her happy and I have blessed you for that. She takes good care of me and I try... Edith has never changed toward me..." William faltered. "I just don't know what I'm going to do now."

"What do you mean?"

"I'm not sure that I can take care of her properly." William lifted his head at that point and repeated. "I don't know if I can cope."

"You must." Frank was concerned but William shook his head.

"You see I have never been much good at it... she has always taken care of me. I can't even boil an egg. Every February, when she went away... with you, she filled the freezer with everything I could possibly need for a month, and arranged all sort of visitors and suchlike. A wonderfully, good woman, Edith is, and when she came back she was glowing and full of life. I was grateful to you, you see... very grateful... but now." William's body shook, and tears of worry and self pity cascaded down his cheeks.

"William you must be strong for Edith now. She needs you... I'll help you."

"What do you mean?"

"I can cook, work a washing machine and an iron. I can show you. I don't live too far away. In fact I could stay for a while with my son in Windermere. I know it is very close to where you live."

114

Frank thought that staying with Jeremy and Simon would be awful but if it meant that he could see Edith, he would cope and perhaps, just perhaps he could get to like Simon a little better. The more he thought about it the better it sounded.

"Are you serious, Frank?" William asked, his face brightening. "Why not stay with us then, we have loads of room. You could move in. We have a lovely house and even though I'm not much good as a housewife, I am pretty handy though: woodwork, plumbing, decorating even though I am a bit slow nowadays. Yes, what a good idea... Perhaps, it could work. The two of us together."

Clasping William's hand, Frank concluded. "We will both look after her then, take turns and keep her happy forever. We can do it together. Yes definitely... Why not? We can do it together, William."

***

SALLY & BEN – A Day at the Beach

"Is it alright, do you think?" Sally asked, turning to Ben who was surveying the line of waiting taxis to see if there was an alternative to the battered, pea-green sardine can that had pulled up in front of them.

An officious little supervisor had pushed them towards it as they had walked out into the blazing sunshine from the covered market place where they had been meandering around for the past hour. They had not intended to stay so long but the spice stalls, the reggae music and the girls in their traditional Creole dresses had held them entranced and now all the regular taxis had disappeared.

"Let's go and find a beach that's not covered in tourists. Perhaps somewhere where we can go skinny-dipping?" Sally said with a suggestive smile, that morning as they prepared to disembark in Guadeloupe. "After all we are on an anniversary cruise, and we haven't done anything naughty for years. What do you say? But after we've done a bit of shopping. We'll go down past the Caravelle Beach where everyone else goes and find a little place that doesn't have burger bars and ice cream vendors."

"Great, not sure about the skinny-dipping though, we might get arrested but yeah, let's do it." Ben replied, visualising Sally's pert little bottom as she ran toward the sea.

It seemed a great idea at the time as they had done the scheduled tours, tourist beaches, markets and 'places of interest' on the other islands that they had visited. Perhaps it was the day to spend time together. Since having their son, Nathan, ten years before they had not had a holiday and this was an opportunity to spice up their love life with a little fun time.

On reading the 'Horizon' magazine that arrived in their cabin daily with all the news, getting a taxi or a bus was not a problem. It was however suggested that they be official rather than the private cabs used on the island and the rate should be agreed before setting off.

Ben had poo-pooed that advice, after all it was a French island and he could speak enough of the lingo to do a little bargaining. He had already practiced that morning as he bought Sally a new watch, and some rather snazzy gold cufflinks for his father's Christmas present. Ben was rather pleased with himself because he got them for at least half the price originally quoted. So he thought anyway!

By the time they had walked through the duty-free shops and into the town market, all the buses and regular taxis seemed to have disappeared but they both felt pretty confident about travelling around to see if they could find a nice little secluded beach all to themselves.

One glance at the driver and Sally looked worried. Ben didn't seem too sure either but he didn't want to worry Sally any more than necessary. A decision not to do one of the accompanied tours now seemed like a really bad idea. Ben grabbed her hand and grinning, moved toward the taxi.

"Quel est le prix pour nous prends vers la bas de la dernière côte Caravelle," asked Ben.

Their driver was young, small and beady-eyed with

a head full of dreadlocks.

"I speak Inglish. I take you to a 'perfik' place for fifteen Euros. 'Perfik' for honeymooner's even." He slapped his lips together in the most suggestive way.

"Oh, ha. ha. He thinks we are on our honeymoon," chuckled Sally.

"Good then he'll definitely take us somewhere off the beaten track," Ben said patting Sally's bum and nodded his agreement.

'Dreadlocks grinned as he opened the door, then leapt into his seat, wriggled down, grasped the steering wheel in a ten-to-two position and stuck out his elbows. Sally thought he was going to shout "brum brum". He reminded her of their ten-year-old son in a bumper car at the fair.

There were no seatbelts and as the taxi leapt forward, Ben and Sally both slid downward. The seats were covered with a slippery nylon cloth and as they hurtled off into the traffic it was difficult not slide about. Every vehicle beeped the horns and their driver was no exception. Pedestrians and the numerous bike riders, weaved in and out of the traffic, an accident waiting to happen.

Their driver obviously had some sort of death wish because he overtook on blind bends and even straight into the oncoming traffic. Other battered taxis, hurtling lorries, overcrowded buses all seemed to be directly ahead of their rattling box on wheels, and as they swung left and right, while Ben and Sally continued to slither around on the nylon blanket. At one point, they approached some roadworks where ten or so workmen and women in brightly coloured overalls and baseball caps were digging a large hole in the road. Heading straight for them and turning at the very last second Ben and Sally's taxi skimmed a few bottoms and blew a great cloud of dust over the workers.

Gripping Ben's hand so that it was impossible for any blood to circulate, Sally repeatedly squeaked, "Oh my God, oh my God," then squeezed her eyes shut.

All she could think was that He obviously wasn't listening! God that is! She tried to remember what a good life she had had and if it was really her destiny to die in the Caribbean, how on earth would their boy manage when their bodies were returned home.

"You pay mo' if you mek noise!" shouted the brown-monkey-daredevil driving their taxi. "I good driver, never fear."

Skidding and sliding, horn blasting, they entered a small market town, but slow down he did not. Parasols, carts and assorted stalls were brushed backward as the taxi careered onward.

Having all the car windows open, the wind whipped Sally's hair into a swirling candy-floss, and every time she opened her mouth with another expletive, she got a mouth full of hair plus a good amount of dust from the road. Spitting and spluttering, Sally appealed to her husband to tell the driver to stop but Ben grinned at her discomfort, held her hand a little more tightly and remained placid and calm throughout the entire journey. He was very philosophical about such things!

Through fields of sugar cane, up and down the mountain roads they careered, bumping and banging all the way, eventually screeching to a halt in a dusty car park several miles down the coast from Caravelle.

"Well, that was fun," laughed Ben, stretching his long legs and dusting himself down. By a miracle they had arrived safely at their destination and that was all that mattered.

"No it wasn't fun. It was terrible and you can only laugh," said Sally hoisting the P&O beach bag over her shoulder.

"We both couldn't get hysterical, could we?"

"How are we going to get back? I swear I'm never going to set foot in another taxi again. Even if I have to walk." Sally was trying to brush the dust from her face and hair but Ben wasn't listening. He was busy rattling through his pockets to find fifteen Euros to give to 'Dreadlocks' when, from a small copse of trees behind him, two other almost identical 'Dreadlocks' appeared, one carrying a rather rusty machete.

"Ben… "

"Have you got a five, Sal?"

"Ben… " The urgency of Sally's voice made Ben look up just as the tallest of the two men arm-locked Ben around the neck. Falling backward, he realised the situation, elbowed his attacker until he let go. Ben was a well built, physically fit man so swivelling onto his knees, he punched the side of his assailant's face hard with his fist. Blood spurted from his cheek and squealing like a smacked piglet, he jumped up and backed away from Ben.

Sally had started to scream as their obnoxious little taxi driver leapt toward her with a warning. "I tol' you not to mek noise."

Pulling her toward him 'Dreadlocks' wrapped his dirty brown arms around her waist and held her in a vice-like hold. Before Ben could get to Sally, Mr-Machete-man had grabbed her hair and held the weapon across her throat and his assailant had rushed to stand behind them, blood still dripping from his face.

Glaring at Ben and daring him to move, 'Dreadlocks' thrust his pelvis into Sally's backside and with a dirty grin moved against her.

Ben stood still, bile rising in his throat and watched Sally's terrified face.

"Let go of my wife. What do you want? You can have every penny we have... anything... let go of her." He pulled money from his wallet, quite a large amount in Euros and a few American dollars, and said, "In the bag there is a watch and cufflinks... Take them and let go of my wife... Lâcher de ma femme."

Mr-Machete-man spoke in rapid French to 'Dreadlocks' who was still gyrating against Sally's backside.

"Juste obtenir leur argent et de la laisses seule... obtenir leur argent."

Dreadlocks stopped pressing into Sally at the sight of the money, "Get t'e bag then."

Ben moved slowly forward and picked up the beach bag just as a large black taxi screeched into the car park, and came to a shuddering halt beside Sally and the 'Dreadlocks' gang. Dust flew everywhere and panic ensued. Sally released, slid down in a faint, Ben swung the beach bag and clouted 'Dreadlocks' as he turned to run back toward the copse from where his cohorts had originally appeared.

Out of the taxi jumped two men who were both waving golf clubs and they chased the three attackers who were shrieking obscenities in French. Just behind the copse, a police car was waiting for them but Ben and

Sally, both covered with dusty sand were unaware of the arrests taking place, as they were busy recovering from their ordeal. Sally sobbed loudly, Ben held her close whilst his beating heart slowed down.

What on earth had just happened? Who were their noble rescuers?

As the two potential golfers returned, grinning and out of breath, Ben held out his hand to thank them. "Guys where did you come from? Thank you so much — -"

"Batman and Robin to the rescue!" yelled the dark good-looking one waving his golf club, whilst the smaller, older rescuer asked, "Are you OK? Good job we spotted you, heh? Glen Lucas, cruise director, and this is Daniel Morreneo, singer and entertainer."

Pumping their hands, Ben thanked them over and over again.

"Ben and Sally Evans. How did you know we were in trouble?"

"We saw you get into the taxi, knew you were one of ours from the beach bag, and the taxi, pretty easily spotted; the Kermit green. Bit of a gang that lot... and we know that another couple from our last cruise had been robbed after riding a green taxi. It was right here that they were robbed, so we knew where to come to."

Ben looked toward the copse, expecting the robbers to return at any moment but instead a burly police officer walked toward them.

"It's OK, they are under arrest now," said Glen noticing Ben's concern. "They will want a statement though. We called them on their way and give 'em their due, they responded straight away. Got the little buggers, bloody menace their sort, but we don't get *too* much

123

trouble here. This is one of the best islands; very little crime usually. "

Statements taken and a lot of hand shaking later, Ben and Sally accompanied their rescuers back to the cruise ship, knowing that they would be more careful in future and stay with the crowd rather than wandering off alone. After all a lot of trouble was taken in organising trips so that passengers could see the islands *and* be safe.

Both Glen and Daniel were entertainers and they liked applause, so their exploits were included in the evening entertainment causing a good deal of praise and laughter. Each reiterated the need to keep to the guidelines and advice given in the 'Horizon' magazine.

Needless to say Ben and Sally applauded the loudest!

***

GISELA – Learning Curve

Just another two bodies to pummel and I will be able to sleep, thought Gisela. Today she was exhausted. A special offer for the day had doubled her turnover of clients.

She had never imagined when she was training that this would be her life for nine months at a time. Endless faceless blobs with cabin numbers passing through her expert hands with no time to talk and get to know her clients. Company policy was just to get through as many treatments as you can, as fast as possible.

Yes, she had a lovely room and an immaculate uniform, and the products they used were sweet smelling and luxurious. The background music was designed to mimic the heartbeat of a relaxed body.

'A bit harder… a bit softer… more there… can you do a bit longer and do you do extras'? questions she heard every single day. 'Is that hard / soft enough? is that the spot? I have another appointment, I'm sorry and no, I definitely don't do extras' were her answers every day too. She made special note of the men who made requests for extras, and made sure that big German Helga got them next time. She definitely didn't do extras, but could massage them into a pulp. That would sort them.

But, this was *not* what she trained so hard for, took all those massage, anatomy and physiology, botany and science exams for. It all seemed a like a distant world. Her ideals of helping people back to health, encouraging and advising them, as her training had included, seemed dimmed to the point of extinction. Being a good masseuse was far more than rubbing down body after body with ready-mixed oils. She had been trained to give every single person an individual prescription of specifically-selected and cross-referenced essential oils in a base oil that was also carefully chosen for each skin type and need. Her teacher at the 'The Rainbow Bridge School' had emphasised that every client should be treated as an individual, but on board ship it was *all* about making money. Gisela moved mechanically through each day repeating her well-exercised routine to the point where she could have done it in her sleep, and hardly being able to recognise one body from the next.

I suppose I must see this as part of my training, she thought. The time spent on the cruise ships was her passport to opening her own clinic back in either Portugal, her home, or Newcastle where she had lived and studied for the preceding three years. The experience itself would constantly remind her of the fine line between being a great therapist and having to pay the rent.

Today her back ached and everyone had lost an hour on the clock as the ship returned through the time zones. It was also the first time she had been seasick. This was her fifth voyage and without doubt her worst. The storms when they had left Southampton had lain her on her back for two days and then again with the rough sea when they had left Antigua, she had spent another day in bed.

As her colleague Jasmine had filled in for her, Gisela had to take some of her appointments to make up her own quota. Perhaps she wasn't really cut out for this life after all. But it was only a means to an end after all. The whole idea was to make enough money to save up for her future, to see a bit of the world but other than a quick run to the shops and the internet cafe. She had actually seen little of the places they had visited. She knew their names of course: Madeira, Barbados, Tortola, St Kitts, St Barts etc etc. They all merged into one as her days were filled with body after body, no time to talk, no time to understand or give advice.

Looking at her appointments for the next two hours she noticed that Miss Betty James was coming for another treatment. A really nice lady who had a muscle-wasting disease, and Gisela remembered her because she had struggled to get on the bed, and at the end of her treatment Betty had turned and hugged her warmly, thanking her profusely.

Oh dear, Gisela thought, *I must do my best for her. It must be so terrible to have a health problem over which you have no control. I must give this unfortunate lady a good treatment. I'll take a painkiller and I'll be fine.*

In the meantime she had a new client, John McDonald, sixty one, neck tension and in need of general relaxation, so his entrance form indicated. He arrived early and with a sheepish grin, followed her into the treatment room.

"First time, you know. Never had a massage before. Quite a treat for me... but as it's on special... well, you know, I thought why not give it a try, eh? Do I get undressed straight away? Yes, OK, will do." he said as Gisela nodded and indicated that he get on the bed. She left the room to wash her hands and collect fresh towels.

On returning John was laid on his back, stark naked, eyes closed and his penis pointing in a straight line up to the ceiling.

Oh, dear God, I've had enough of this. thought Gisela and plonked the two folded towels straight on top of the quivering tool as if she hadn't noticed it. His body folded and his head shot off the bed but Gisela turned her back. "Turn onto your stomach, please Mr McDonald, and put your face into the hole in the bed."

As soon as he had done so and wriggled his equipment into a comfortable position, she gave him the worst massage that she had ever performed with a good bit of slapping and hacking and without asking him to turn over, all the time humming along to the music.

At the end of the forty-five minutes she whipped the towels off him, and said charmingly, "Right, Mr McDonald, you're done, off you go. Enjoy the rest of your day."

She marched out of the treatment room, depositing the towels in the dirty linen box on her way to the staff room where she made herself a cup of much-needed chamomile tea and took a pain killer. She had fifteen minutes until her next client.

Welcoming Miss Betty later, Gisela was calm and ready to do her very best. She was immediately struck by Miss Betty's smile. It lit up her lined face life a ray of sunlight off the sea.

"Hello dear girl, so lovely to see you again. Gisela, my dear, I can't tell you how much your treatment did for me last week. I have never felt better, even managed some deck quoits, and my shoulders haven't been so mobile in years. You have done wonders."

Gisela smiled and glowed inwardly. What a good feeling. After all, she still had the power to help whoever crossed her path, even though she felt that she wasn't giving as much as she should. She was so grateful to Miss Betty that she resolved from that moment on to see her job in a different light. Bugger the Mr McDonalds of the world!

"Right let's see what we can do for you today Miss Betty, then perhaps you can try swimming this week."

***

SILVYA & RUKA – Going Home

Ruka knocked discreetly on the door of cabin 762 but could hear no sound, and the instruction card had not been left out in its usual place. Should he wait or knock again? He knew he must take care not to invade the privacy of his charges, but it was getting late and the cabin needed servicing. He was a long-serving cabin boy, sadly no longer a boy. He would be fifty-three next birthday and he had worked on all the cruisers since his twenty-first year. It seemed to him now that this was all that remained of his life: taking care of people regardless of how he was treated and sending his earnings back to India to help educate his sister's five children and support their disabled brother, none of whom he had seen for over two years. Ruka was a good Christian man and considered himself extremely lucky, to not only be employed but of being in very good health.

Mrs Silvya Bartholomy in 762 was a delight to attend and it made Ruka realise that he was indeed serving his Lord in his daily work. Ruka had met Silvya on her first cruise around the world and over the years that followed, he had become rather fond of her. He had seen her on many cruises since then and had learned a great deal about her life and she about his. She had listened carefully when he told her of his younger widowed sister and how she struggled with five children to educate and how his disabled brother needed constant care.

When not cruising, Silvya had kept in touch, sending him postcards with pictures of the sights of London: the Houses of Parliament, Tower Bridge, St

Paul's Cathedral, and even one of a London bus. She knew that Ruka had never had time to visit the sights, and only really ever saw Heathrow airport on his way back to India.

He carefully stored the cards and took them home to his nieces and nephews when he returned on leave.

Once again, Silvya had booked this particular Caribbean cruise because he would be on it and that somehow she had manipulated her cabin number to be on his round and he was always very pleased to see her. His kindness to her had not gone unnoticed and Silvya Bartholomy appreciated his gentle ways and genuine concern.

"Hello, Mrs Bartholomy. Are you there?" he called, preparing to use his key if he got no answer.

"Come in, Ruka. I'm ready now," replied the small, refined voice, and opening the door, she said, "It's really very kind of you to come and visit me."

"It's my job to visit you and clean your room," he smiled. It was part of their routine to be very business-like whilst he was still on duty.

"Oh I think it's been done already, thank you," she replied emphasising the fact with her little shrivelled brown hands that everything was clean, neat, tidy and folded. She was a diminutive woman with a round, bony chin and soft white curls. Her hands flapped to and fro like little birds, flicking this way and that as she spoke. She finally patted the seat beside her. "Do come in and take tea with me."

"I cannot, Madam, I have to finish my shift."

"I will wait then. Please come, I have some Earl Grey."

"You know I only drink coffee, Madam."

"You should try it. My father would never drink anything but Yorkshire tea until he tried it," she replied, her pale-blue rheumy eyes twinkling. "My father was a miner you know. He'd drink his Earl Grey with me perched on his lap and every Friday we would sit together and pick out the numbers for his pools, his football pools... Do you have them in India?"

Ruka nodded.

"We would discuss what we would do if he won. Sounds silly now, but I would sit on his knee putting the crosses in place and make wonderful plans: to go to Poland where my mother was born, around the world in eighty days, or buy a huge house so I could have a horse.

Ruka watched how expressively Mrs Bartholomy used her hands, miming little movement as she talked, her thumb and forefinger together indicating the crosses of which she spoke and then folding her fingers into fists as if she was holding the reins of a horse. He found her a very charming person.

Ruka had spent time with Mrs Bartholomy on every one of the eighteen days that they had been at sea, except for the day that she had gone on a coach trip around Barbados. He had even managed to accompany her on a shopping trip in Tortola where she had insisted on buying gifts for him to take home for his family.

"I have no one to buy for and need nothing for myself so you must let me have the pleasure." She had insisted as she paid for several extremely nice blouses, a length of lovely cotton material and hair combs for his sister, a kite, a skateboard, a little dolls house and several other toys for his nephews and nieces.

Ruka was overwhelmed with her generosity and

133

resolved that she should want for nothing on their return trip to Southampton, where they would start their next trip to the Mediterranean. He hoped sincerely that that he would be able to be with her.

They were now firm friends so he would make every effort to come back later that day although it was probably impossible because. "I will try, Madam, but I have laundry duty today. Do you have any to take?"

"No, thank you, Ruka. I hope to see you tomorrow then."

"Definitely, Madam," he said as he closed the door behind him, only having added an extra toilet roll and smoothed the covers of her immaculately-tidy bed.

Silvya smiled to herself knowing that he would return if he could. He was such a good man; he arranged anything she wanted, collected her medicines and brought her special pastries from the kitchen. She had a penchant for little almond macaroons and Ruka had some specially made for her in the staff kitchens downstairs.

On every cruise, without instruction, he would take it upon himself to check on Silvya whenever his shifts allowed. He knew that she was frail and needed lots of medication.

This week he had noticed how swollen her legs were and that she often held her little hand to her heart as she rose from her chair, her breath wheezing slightly and her brows creasing as if in pain, but she never complained. Yes, he would definitely return when he could.

Silvya felt like a worn out clock, winding slowly down until the time would come when, the hands would still, and all that would left would be the echo of the past. Nevertheless, the vein of happiness that ran through Silvya today was in the knowledge that she wouldn't be alone. She could walk, even though it be slowly, or sit, join in, or not with the plethora of whist drives, bridge or bingo, she could talk to people or not, eat as and when she was ready without worrying about shopping or cooking, she could go to one of the interesting lectures, watch a film, look out across the sea or sit in the library reading, but she would never be alone here. That was the reason that it was the sixth year of cruising that Silvya had enjoyed. She was eighty-eight and had recently sold her house in Muswell Hill so that she could cruise full-time. She has reckoned that she had enough money to last until she was ninety-nine with plenty to spare if the prices didn't escalate, and she continued to get the reductions for booking another trip on every cruise. But, she would not need to book that far ahead as she knew that she it was unlikely that she would need that much time. Perhaps one more year, perhaps less.

Her own doctor had confirmed just a month before, what she had already really known. She had 'senile aortic stenosis heart disease' and it was only a matter of time before her old ticker stopped completely. She had undergone several surgeries which catheterised the arteries, *and* had angioplasty, both of which had resulted in scarring of the heart mechanisms. No further intervention was possible. She knew that the condition could deteriorate very quickly and that it could be very painful so she had made provisions to speed her own death when it became necessary.

She had not declared her medical condition when she booked the latest Caribbean adventure, but she had carefully researched and knew that death at sea was not uncommon and that every large ship had a morgue and that they would take care of all the arrangements to have her body returned home if necessary.

As she checked the time and fished her handbag from the tiny wardrobe her thoughts confirmed her decision. *Everything is here. If I need more medication it can be obtained for a small sum. All my laundry is taken care of and returned beautifully ironed. No need to worry about doctor's appointments or having enough to eat. If the weather is bad I don't have to worry about heating bills. Everything on board is controlled to be comfortable whether in the Caribbean heat or the Canadian ice. At home I might have to do without both my medication and a sufficient amount of heating if the weather got really bad.*

It is indeed such a bore getting old. In my own eyes, I'm not really very old but my mind and my body are no longer in sync. In my head, I am capable of almost anything that I could do at twenty, but sadly even when my head says I can, my body refuses, weakens and complains. Just lately rising from any chair necessitates a certain amount of balance and negotiating. Still I am prepared for the worst. All my affairs are in order, all I own now is in this cabin and will easily fit into my two suitcases. My will has been taken care of too and a copy is safely tucked into my bedside drawer next to my collection of sleeping pills that will take me on my final journey if and when it becomes necessary. I have time to make a few more memories as we will be docking in Ponta Delgada in a few days and I intend to make the best of it.

Memories – they are all I have now. The young

have futures, full of hopes and dreams, while the old hold the remains of their life in their hands and wonder where all the years went.

Her thought were without bitterness as looking back at her reckless youth, the tragic years through the war, the passions, the feckless love affairs, the lovely child who died before he was three, and the lonely, solitary, years that had passed since her husband George had died she had lived a full life. Yes, she would say she had lived; carefully at times, but if not to the full, at least to the brim. She had travelled and been relatively successful in most things that she had tried. She had a few secrets too.

No time to waste. I think I will go and join the art group if I can get there before they start.

It was well past midnight and Ruka knelt to say his prayers. He was so tired but he would not forsake his time with his Lord. He prayed for his brother that he might have the strength and will to overcome his pain and be able to enjoy the short time he had left. Ruka also prayed fervently that his sister's second daughter become less wilful and help her mother more.

"Please keep them all well and safe, Lord so that I can help them when I get my leave after the next trip to the Mediterranean. I will have three months at home with them all, but in the meantime please take care of my family. I also need to have a word to you about my friend Mrs Silvya Bartholomy. She has really got bad and the pain that she is suffering is wearing her down. Can you give her a little assistance please. Thank you Lord. Amen."

Climbing into bed, Ruka resolved that he would

make sure that she went straight to the hospital when she disembarked in Southampton in three days' time for he had spent an hour with her the previous evening and for the first time ever, she had kissed him goodnight, and said, "All will be well, Ruka, don't worry." He had left with a sad heart knowing that she was indeed old and very tired of her pain.

The next morning was dull and foggy, a sure indication that they would soon be arriving back in, England.

Such a grey wet country, thought Ruka. *I will be so glad to get home to India.*

Thinking about arriving in Southampton, he decided to check on Mrs Bartholomy as soon as he had finished his early morning duties; retrieving all the abandoned trays, collecting shoes and laundry and distributing the morning information.

His arrival at her cabin confirmed his suspicion that all was not well and he carefully opened her door. He could see propped on her dressing table the little water colour painting that she had finished the previous day. It showed a sunlit beach with a palm tree that leant toward the sea. Very pretty, reminding him of home in Panaji.

"Are you sleeping, Mrs Bartholomy?" he inquired, creeping forward so that he could see her bed.

No response. He knew almost instantly that she would not reply.

Her soft white curls were spread across the pillow and she was smiling. She was fully dressed in her very best rose-pink silk blouse and skirt, and she held three letters in her folded hands.

For a short moment, Ruka looked at the sweet face.

She was the kindest person he had ever known. He said a small prayer of thanks, not only for her friendship but for her release. She was at peace now.

About to leave, he noticed the little empty pill bottle by her side. So she really had found the pain too much to bear. He realised too that if there was any question about the cause of her death there would have to be an inquest and he felt in his heart that Silvya wouldn't want that. He carefully pocketed the plastic bottle and assuming the letters were her final instructions and farewells to friends, she had no family that he knew of, he placed them on her dressing table, knowing the captain himself would come and collect them.

Very quickly, wheels were set in motion; the ship's doctor pronounced her dead, most probably from natural causes, the medical staff carefully folded her body into a white shroud and her body was transferred to the morgue.

Ruka had wept as he locked her cabin door and found it difficult to continue with his duties so he went below deck and made himself a coffee. He went to his tiny bunk, and laying the coffee to one side, he put his hands together and asked his Lord to give his dear friend Mrs Silvya Bartholomy a happy and safe journey to His side.

It was early evening when Captain Johnston called Ruka to his office and informed him that one of the letters from Mrs Bartholomy's cabin was addressed to him and the captain duly handed it over. Ruka was apprehensive about opening it before his evening duties, so resolved to read it when he went to bed so that he could mourn his dear friend privately. There were always so many people around and so much activity at that time of the day. Passengers off to the dining rooms to get an early dinner before the shows, waiters hurrying through corridors with cocktails and dinner orders, clothes being returned from the laundry, so much going on that it seemed the right thing to do so he tucked the letter under his pillow and fulfilled his evening duties as fast as he could.

It was well past one am when he finally pulled on his 'kurta' and opened the letter. It was several pages long and written on soft blue airmail paper. It smelt of lily-of-the-valley, her favourite fragrance. Adjusting his small light, he read:

My Dear Ruka
If you are reading this you will know that I have left this earthly plain to travel onward into the unknown. My infirmities have reached a point that I can no longer bear and I do not want to be carted off to a home or hospital and just become a burden to others. Unlike you I have little faith left in God but I do think that perhaps there is something after life on earth.

I want to thank you for your incredible kindness in the few years I have known you. You have always been genuinely good to me and I want you to know how much that has meant to me. I have told you about my only son Joseph, haven't I ? If he hadn't died so young he would be the same age as you are now and I like to think that he would have been as honourable and caring to me as you have been to your family. Your presence in my life has always brought such pleasure and hearing about your family has made me realise what an unselfish man you are. It is time you retired and took pleasure in your home country for which I know you yearn.

Today is my eighty-ninth birthday and that is an astonishing amount of time to live, even in this age of wonders. As you know, I have had an interesting and full life but there are a few things you do not know about me which I will explain later.

Firstly I must tell you of my plans for you. On return to Southampton I wish you to contact my solicitor in London who has my final will and testament. Messrs Jones and Son. 51, Trensitt St, London N10 7ER. Telephone number on envelope. He will know who you are.

I have left you enough money to go home and look after you brother and sister's family and so that you can live comfortably for the rest of your life, perhaps even take a wife as I know that the lack of which is one of your regrets.

Now I must tell you how this daughter of a simple miner came to have such a fortune to give away.

In 1925, when I was born, my mother Alina was employed by Heniek Spasowski, a Polish artist and draughtsman who had employed her since her tenth birthday as a maid for his wife Maria. Alina had no living family and had been in an orphanage since she was five years old. She considered herself very lucky to be employed by a family who were not only kind to her but fed her well and travelled a great deal. My mother's horizons changed almost overnight as Heniek Spasowski was a gifted man, commissioned for work on large buildings and in manufacturing industries all over the world.

In 1920, my mother was residing in India with the family in a small house somewhere in Southern India (I do not remember exactly where but I do remember that you came from somewhere in the Southwest) because Heniek had got a commission to design advertising and posters for the new railway system.

Whilst in India, Heniek saw the opportunity to invest in the growing cotton industry. The labour, much of which was by young children, was cheap. (I tell you all this because it has a bearing on one of the many reasons I want you to have this money.)

By exploiting this workforce, huge profits could be made. He added to their designs which were so successful that he decided to export some of the products to Europe. So, explaining how he came to be in England with his wife and my mother in 1923-25...

His import / export business thrived and he became a rich man. He settled in England for a while as the majority of his exports went there.

I do not know for how long his relationship with my mother had gone on but I do know that when she became pregnant in 1924 he virtually abandoned her in the North of England and departed back to India. She gave birth to me in a workhouse in Leeds and only by real luck, she managed to secure a job as housemaid in the employ of a coal mine owner named Thomas Growther who allowed her to bring me with her to his great house in Sunderland. This is where she met and married my father.

I did not know that he wasn't my real father until after his death in the war in 1940. For four years we struggled without him but after the war was over, we had a letter from Heniek Spasowski's solicitor informing us that he was dead and had left all his money to me, his only child. Overnight I became a rich young lady and my mother told me all about him. I think she had loved him in a way but gratitude for rescuing her from the orphanage in Poland a greater part of her feelings toward him, I am sure.

As I was explaining, my real father Heniek took a great deal from your country at the expense of the workforce, many of whom died in his employ because of the awful working conditions in which they worked. He never did improve them as I learnt when I went to India myself many years later. I heard some very sad stories born out of poverty and neglect in the cotton mills.

You can perhaps now see how you, with your kindness and friendship, have implemented a situation whereby I can return some of his money back to India via your needs for your own family.

I have no family and to know that you and yours are happy and taken care of has given me such a good feeling that I have no regrets in departing slightly sooner than I was perhaps destined to.

Thank you again, dearest Ruka. I wish you a long and happy life and perhaps if there is a heaven I will see you there.

Your Friend
Silvya Bartholomy.

Ps. The sum is in the excess of 400,000.00 pounds so if you don't need it all please do donate it to any charity that helps poor workers, perhaps even in the cotton industry.

Ruka was shaken by her letter, and knew that with that amount of money, he would be able to make a difference to so many lives. To go home and stay was his dream and it really *was* going to happen. Such happiness it would bring to his family and he would have enough money and time to help others in need too. He would of course stay in London for a while until everything was sorted out, and perhaps see some of the sights from the postcards that Silvya had sent him over the years.

He decided that his retirement bonus for his long service would be donated to the charity that funds research into heart disease. So many decisions, so many choices that the money would give him.

Thank you, Mrs Silvya Bartholomy. My pleasure in serving you has been immense, I will not let you down. Rest in Peace.

*** ***

About the Author

Joy Burnett is a well-travelled, independent lady who loves new experiences. Having lived in Oman, Brunei, Abu Dhabi and Spain, she now lives in Northamptonshire, UK.

On retirement, she joined a local writers group, which inspired her to start writing novels, her first of which is 'On the Loose', and she is already planning others.

Her professional life included fashion retail management, aromatherapy, reflexology and nutrition.

For eleven years, she taught and practiced natural medicine in her own school in North Yorkshire.

She now enjoys her pets, painting and local theatre.

***

Note from the Author

Thank you for downloading 'All at Sea'. I hope you enjoyed it and would be very grateful if you would leave a review. Thank you.

If you would like to know more about my writing, I would love to hear from you. My email address is joyburnettwriter@yahoo.co.uk.

Made in the USA
Columbia, SC
17 July 2018